Copyright © 2021 by Jade Ember

All rights reserved.

No part of this publication may be reproduced, distributed, or transmitted in any form or by any means, including photocopying, recording, or other electronic or mechanical methods, without the prior written permission of the publisher, except as permitted by U.S. copyright law.

The story, all names, characters, and incidents portrayed in this production are fictitious. No identification with actual persons (living or deceased), places, buildings, and products is intended or should be inferred.

Book Cover by: GetCovers

CLAIMING MY WOLF

JADE EMBER

Chapter One

~~Sadie's PoV~~

"Sadie! Hurry up, you're going to be late!"

I groan as my aunt's voice echoes up the stairs. I'm already ready, I've been ready for ten minutes at least, I just don't want to go.

I don't want to go to a new school. I don't want to be the new girl, the one everyone stares at. And I really don't want to be the girl with the dead parents that everyone feels sorry for.

But that's my life, and sitting alone in my room won't change it, so I get up and go downstairs where my cousins Aaron and Ava are waiting.

We all get in Aaron's car. He and Ava are twins and they're two months older than me. They'll be 18 in just a few days and they're really excited about it. Like, ridiculously excited. I sort of get it, it's fun to be an adult and all, but they act like their whole lives are going to change. In my head, I think it's just another birthday, but I don't say it out loud. Just because I don't have any reason to smile these days doesn't mean I have to rain on their parade.

"You're going to love Westbridge High," Ava tells me from the front seat as we drive across town. "There are so many hot guys, you won't know which way to look first."

"Really, Ava?" Aaron asks, rolling his eyes at his sister. "If I said that about the girls, you'd call me a pig."

"There's nothing wrong with looking," she retorts, sticking her tongue out at him. "Just because you've been in love with the same girl forever doesn't mean the rest of us are ready to settle down yet."

Aaron's face softens at the mention of his girlfriend Laurel. I've already met her, she's been at their house every day since I arrived a week ago. She's nice, though I haven't talked to her much. I haven't talked to anyone much.

I haven't felt much like talking.

"Besides," Ava continues, still chatting away merrily. "Sadie needs to have some fun before she's eighteen, you never know when she'll find her ma... ow!"

She breaks off as Aaron punches her arm, giving her a warning glare.

"My what?" I pipe up, curious about what she was going to say, but Ava just laughs nervously.

"Nothing, never mind. Come on, let's go and meet everyone!"

I look out the window and see that we've arrived at the school. It's a two-story building with a big flight of steps up to the front door. Students are milling around outside and nobody seems to be in a hurry to go in even though it's pretty cold out. It's March and the snow has just started to melt.

The snow that caused my parent's accident.

That now-familiar sense of loss stabs at me, but I force myself to push it down and put something close to a smile on my face as we get out of the car and walk towards a group of people about our age. There are some really pretty girls, and, as Ava promised, some really hot guys too. I have to stop my mouth from falling open as I get my first real look at some of them.

Is this some kind of supermodel school? I've never seen so many good-looking people in one place in my whole life.

"Hey everyone!" Ava exclaims as we walk up to the group. Of course, she fits right in with all the beautiful people with her gently curling blonde hair and bright blue eyes. "This is my cousin Sadie. She's going to be going to school here for the rest of the year."

Everyone turns to look at me all at once and I'm suddenly very aware of just how ordinary I am compared to all of them. "Hi," I manage to say. "Nice to meet you."

One of the guys steps forward and my heart immediately starts beating faster. Holy crap on a stick, he is gorgeous. Dark hair and piercing green eyes, a strong jaw and biceps straining against his shirt so hard that I'm amazed it hasn't given up the fight yet and just ripped right off him.

I try to smile as he stares at me, but the words out of his mouth quickly kill off any small hopes I might have that he was actually interested in me.

"Is this a joke, Ava?" he asks, even though he's still looking right at me. "I already told you, we don't want her kind here."

My *kind*? What is that supposed to mean?

"Oh, I'm sorry." The words are out of my mouth before I even know I thought them. "I didn't realize only assholes were allowed to go here."

There are surprised glances and a few nervous laughs among the others, but the guy in front of me just narrows his eyes at me. "Someone needs to show you your place, little mutt."

Did he actually just call me a fucking mutt? What the hell?

Before I can say anything else, the bell rings and everyone heads inside. Ava grabs my arm and pulls me along with her, away from Mr High-and-Mighty.

"Sorry about that," she tells me as we get inside the warm hallway. "Micah takes some warming up, but he's not so bad when you get to know him. Just try to stay away from him for a little while, okay?"

I don't want to get to know him after that introduction, but I don't tell Ava that now. I let her pull me down the hall to an open door, where she pushes me inside with my bookbag.

"This is your homeroom. I'm just across the hall if you need me, but Mr Latham will probably give you a buddy to show you around. He's really nice, so don't worry. I'll see you at lunch, okay? Have a good morning, Sadie!"

With that, she heads out the door and I'm left alone in my new homeroom with my new classmates who are all staring at me like something's growing out of my head.

I head towards an empty desk and give the girl next to it a tentative smile. "Is this free?"

She just shrugs at me, which I take as a yes, so I sit down and take out a notebook and pen. The last few desks fill up until there's only one left, the one right on the other side of me. Finally, a man in a sweater vest and khakis comes in and I figure this must be Mr Latham. He's about to start talking when the door opens again and the gorgeous jerk from earlier, Micah, walks in.

He spies the open desk and me next to it, and his face immediately darkens to a scowl.

"Sit down, Mr Geary," Mr Latham says. "And try to be on time next time."

Micah walks over and throws himself into the seat, pulling the desk a little farther away from me as he sits.

What the hell is this guy's problem?

"I'm sure you've all noticed we have a new student joining us today," Mr Latham says, giving me a warm smile. At least *he* seems to be happy that I'm here. "Sadie, do you want to tell us a little about yourself?"

Ava warned me this might happen, so at least I'm a little prepared. I stay sitting but look around the room as confidently as I can, looking at everyone except Micah. "Hey, I'm Sadie. I just moved here to live with my aunt and uncle. My cousins are Aaron and Ava Miller. It's nice to meet you all."

I try to sound sincere, but no one really meets my eye except Mr Latham, who gives me an encouraging nod. "Thanks Sadie. We were all very sorry to hear about your parents, but I hope you'll enjoy living here in our pa... I mean, town."

Everyone already knows about my parents? Tears fill my eyes unexpectedly and I look down, not wanting anyone to notice me getting emotional. And what was he about to say at the end before he changed his mind? It isn't the first time that's happened. Several times since I got here, people will start to say something and change the word halfway through.

At first, I thought I was imagining things, but it's happened so many times now that I'm pretty sure it's not just me.

All I can think right now is that this is not at all the way I thought my senior year was going to go. I wish this was all a bad dream and I could wake up back in my bed at home with my parents downstairs and my old friends waiting at my old school and everything would be like it was before.

But that's never going to happen, so I'm just going to have to make the best of where I am, even if it means being in this strange school full of super-hot people, sitting next to a jerk like Micah Geary.

~~Ava's PoV~~

It's lunchtime before I see Sadie again. She looks a little sad, but not as bad as when she first got here. Hopefully, school is helping to take her mind off her parents and leaving behind all her friends. I can't imagine what she's going through but I'm trying to help by just being as normal as I can and not treating her like there's anything wrong with her.

That's easier said than done when jerks like Micah nearly blow it right off the bat.

We had a big school assembly last week to make sure everyone knew about Sadie and how to act around her until my aunt and uncle break the news to her about what we all are and what she is too, even though she doesn't know it.

We're all werewolves.

I can't imagine not knowing. I grew up here in the Westbridge Pack where everyone is a werewolf. It's completely normal. From the time we're pups, we're taught about ranks and mates and everything to do with pack life.

But Sadie's mom, my aunt Cathy, found a human mate, and there were a lot of the pack that didn't accept that at the time. Rather than deal with the constant harassment, they decided to move away to a human city, and Sadie was raised as a human. The few times she came to visit, we stayed in our house so she didn't see anyone else from the pack. But she hardly ever came to visit; most of the time, we went to visit them.

Now, her parents are dead and she has no other family, and she's going to turn 18 soon anyway, so it's better that she's here in the pack for when she meets her wolf and shifts for the first time and everything else, but wow, it's going to be a lot for her to deal with. I don't think she even knows that werewolves are real, never mind that she is one!

And even though attitudes have improved since my aunt found her human mate, there are still some idiots like Micah Geary who think that being half-human is something to be ashamed of. If he wasn't the son of our pack's Beta, I'd have punched him in the junk for speaking to Sadie like that this morning.

"Sadie!" I call out to get her attention and she looks over at me and smiles in relief. "Grab your lunch, we've got a table over here."

I point to the table where me and my friends always eat lunch. Aaron and Laurel are already there along with a few others. Sadie nods and heads for the lunch line while I go take a seat next to Aaron.

"You need to talk to Micah and tell him to back off."

Aaron grimaces. "He won't listen to me."

That's true. Micah thinks he's better than everyone else, except the one person in school who outranks him.

"Then talk to Logan."

We both turn at the same time to look at the table in the corner where we know the Alpha's son will be. Sure enough, he's sitting there all alone, the same as every day, his headphones on, staring at his phone.

The same way he's been for the last year.

"I'm not going to bother Logan with this," Aaron growls. "I'll talk to Micah if I have to. Just don't expect it to do any good."

Sadie walks up with her lunch tray, so we immediately change the subject. I ask her about her classes and introduce her to our other friends. First is Ethan, our Gamma's son, though I don't introduce him to Sadie that way. There's Blair and Tonya, they're both cheerleaders and are dating Micah and Ethan, in that order. Then there's Jordan, Kevin and Adam, they're all on the football team too, along with Aaron.

I secretly hope that Jordan's my mate, though I haven't told anyone that yet. We'll know very soon. He already turned 18 a couple of months ago and hasn't found his mate yet, which probably means it's someone younger. Someone like me, maybe. My birthday is this coming weekend, so we'll find out then, and I cross my fingers under the table as the thought crosses my mind.

My bigger worry, though, is that Aaron and Laurel *won't* be mates. She's already 18 too, so they'll know at our birthday party. If they're not, I don't know what they're going to do. They've been together for years already and they're so ridiculously in love, it makes me a little sick... although, it's probably just jealousy.

All through lunch, I wait for Micah to show up, but he doesn't. That's probably a good thing. We just have to get through a few more days anyway. Mom and Dad have promised that they'll have 'the talk' with Sadie before our birthday party, since we're going to shift there and it would probably majorly freak her out if she didn't know it was coming!

"Who's that over there?" Sadie asks me as we stand up to clear our trays at the end of lunch. I follow her gaze and see that it's Logan she's looking at. I can see why he caught her eye. At a school of hot guys, he's probably the hottest. Or at least he used to be, back when he remembered how to smile.

"His name's Logan," I tell her. "He's lost somebody too, but he's not dealing with it very well. It's better just to stay away from him unless he talks to you first."

She nods, but I'm not totally sure she heard me. She's still staring over at him and I get a bit of a bad feeling about it. Everyone knows not to bother the Alpha's son, but Sadie doesn't even know what an Alpha is, so how can I explain it to her?

The sooner she finds out the truth about all of us, the better.

~~Logan's PoV~~

I don't even hear the bell over the music blaring in my ears. It isn't until someone comes and stands in front of me that I realize that lunch is over and the cafeteria's empty.

It's not the first time it's happened, but it's the first time someone came to check on me.

I look up and see a girl I've never seen before. She's got long dark hair that hangs straight down, some of it's pulled back off her face but from where I'm sitting I can't see how it's tied back. Her eyes are dark too, like her hair, a dark chocolate color that's almost black.

She's just standing there and staring at me, until I start to get a bit annoyed.

"What do you want?" I snap.

"Lunch is over," she says, like it wasn't already obvious. "I thought maybe you didn't hear the bell."

I didn't, but I don't tell her that. I lie instead. "I wasn't ready to go yet."

"Oh. I just thought I'd tell you in case you didn't want to be late for class."

No one would ever say a word about me being late for class, but obviously, this girl doesn't know that. Does she really not know who I am?

Suddenly, I remember that assembly we had last week, about the new girl that was coming who didn't know she was a werewolf. Suddenly, it all made sense. I think they said her parents died or something?

Fuck, if that's true, I don't need to give her a hard time. I have to respect the fact that she's standing here talking to me at all. I guess I could cut her some slack.

"You're new here, right?" I ask as I stand up. Her eyes go a bit wide when she sees how tall I am. It almost makes me laugh, which is weird. I haven't laughed at anything in a long time. She must not have been around any Alphas before.

"R-right," she stutters and takes a step back clumsily, but she seems to get over her surprise. "I'm Sadie."

"Logan." I know I'm not saying much, but honestly, it's the longest conversation I've had with anyone for quite a while. "Why aren't you in class, Sadie?"

She makes a cute little apologetic face. "To be honest, I got lost. I thought I knew where I was going but somehow, I ended up back here. And then I saw you so I came over, but I still don't know where I'm going."

"What class do you have?" I ask, surprised to hear the words coming out of my mouth. Why do I care?

"Math with Mr Craig?" She says it like a question, but lucky for her, I know exactly where it is. It's the class I'm supposed to be in too.

"Come on," I tell her. "I'll show you."

Chapter Two

~~Sadie's PoV~~

I try not to stare at Logan as he walks down the hall just ahead of me. He's so tall and broad, he hardly seems real. He looked way less intimidating when he was sitting at the table, bent over his phone. If I had seen him standing up first, I probably wouldn't have gone over to talk to him.

I'm not even sure why I did. Ava told me to stay away from him and he definitely gave off a 'don't talk to me' vibe. Everyone else gave him a wide berth, but when I found myself back in the cafeteria and saw him sitting there all alone after everyone else had gone, I had an urge to go and make sure that he was okay.

Or at least make sure that he knew that lunch had ended.

It's kind of funny to me that I thought I could help him, now that I see just how little he must need anyone's help.

"In here," he says as he stops outside a classroom door, opening it up and holding it open to let me go first.

He doesn't talk much, I notice, but he's still polite in a kind of old-fashioned way. Like his parents made sure he had good manners.

The thought of his parents leads me to thoughts of my parents, and that same sadness shoots through me. I close my eyes for just a second to try to hold it together.

"Hey, you alright?"

When I open my eyes again, Logan's giving me a curious look, but it's not unfriendly. It's almost sympathetic.

"Fine," I assure him, even though I'm lying. Before he can ask me anything else, I step past him into the room and everyone inside turns to stare.

"Yes?" the tall, thin man at the front of the room asks. He must be Mr Craig. With thin wireframe glasses, he looks exactly like you'd expect a math teacher to look.

"I'm Sadie Jennings, I'm supposed to be in this class," I explain, and his mouth sets in an unimpressed expression.

"Be on time next time, Ms Jennings," he snaps at me, pointing to an empty desk. "Take a seat."

There's a rustling among the other students and I realize Logan has walked in behind me.

"It's my fault Sadie's late," he lies for me, speaking to the teacher. "She was helping me with something."

It's nice of him to try, but I don't expect that will make much difference. But to my surprise, the teacher bends his head to Logan almost submissively. "I didn't realize, Mr Riley. That's fine, then. Please sit down, both of you, when you're ready."

Okay, that's weird. Why would a teacher defer to a student like that? Nobody else acts like it's strange though, so I go sit in the seat that Mr Craig pointed to earlier while Logan heads for an empty one on the other side of the room.

An hour later when the bell rings, I'm completely lost. The stuff they're working on in this class is way different than what I was learning in my old school. I'm going to have to ask Ava or Aaron to help me catch up.

As I pick up my bookbag and shove my notebook inside, a pair of shoes appears beside me. Without even looking up, I know who it is.

"Do you know where your next class is?" Logan asks, and his deep voice makes me shiver. There's something strong and authoritative in it, and I almost feel like bowing down to him like the teacher did.

Why do I feel like that? What is it about this guy?

"Chemistry, I think," I manage to reply, and Logan nods.

"Me too. I'll walk you there."

There's murmuring around us from some of the other kids in the class who must have been listening to what he said. I glance around and, sure enough, several of them are looking at me curiously or whispering to their friends behind their hands.

Is it so strange that Logan would walk with me? I wish I understood what was happening.

He doesn't speak as we make our way through the busy halls. The crowd parts in front of him almost by magic, like there's some kind of force around him that pushes people out of the way. I don't feel that though. I almost feel the opposite, like there's something pulling me to him instead.

Maybe my grief is making me a little crazy. It's the only explanation that makes any sense.

"Logan!" A familiar voice shouts out as we enter the room and my stomach sinks as I see Micah Geary walking over. He spots me too, just a second later, and the grin on his face quickly turns to a scowl.

"Hey, Micah," Logan greets him casually. "Have you met Sadie?"

Micah looks between Logan and me in consternation. "You're hanging out with her?" he asks Logan. I guess it's supposed to be under his breath, but I hear it anyway. "You know what she is, right?"

Logan just raises his eyebrows in challenge. "You mean that she's new here?"

Micah's face scrunches up, looking more confused than ever. "No, I mean she's..."

"Everyone get to your stations," a woman in a white lab coat announces, cutting off whatever Micah's about to say.

Everyone shuffles over to one of the lab stations set up and I just stand there a little awkwardly, not sure where I'm supposed to go.

"You must be Sadie," the teacher says, giving me a warm smile. She's only like the second person today who's actually smiled at me, so I appreciate it. "I'm Ms Browning. Everyone's already paired up with a lab partner for this term, so you can join whichever group you'd like to."

Nothing like putting me on the spot. My eyes flit around the room, trying to decide where to go. Logan seems to be paired up with another guy who's almost as big and really good-looking too. What is with the guys at this school, honestly?

Meanwhile, Micah's still glaring at me from the next table where he's sitting next to a pretty girl who's wearing way too much make-up. She was at our table at lunch but I can't remember her name, and it's not like I'd choose to join Micah's table anyway.

Finally, I go to the front where there are two girls who look relatively normal. "Is it okay if I join you?" I ask.

"Sure," one shrugs, not looking at me, and my stomach sinks again.

But the other one turns to me with a kinder smile. "Of course. You're Sadie, right? I'm Alison and this is Emma. Don't mind her, she's just jealous that Logan walked you to class."

I look at the other girl in surprise and her cheeks are turning red. "I didn't say that! Ally, you're so dead!"

The teacher starts talking again before any of us can say anything else and soon we're working on an experiment and I forget all about the unusually hot guys of Westbridge High. Ally and Emma are funny and smart, and by the time class is over, I'm hopeful we might be friends.

But not today. Today has been a really long day, and I just want to go home and lie on my bed with my pillow over my head for a while.

I say goodbye to my new classmates and head out the door to find Ava, not daring to glance over at either Logan or Micah as I go.

~~Micah's PoV~~

"Come on, baby," Blair coos at me, slipping her hands down the back of my jeans, her fingers warm against my ass. "My parents are going to be back soon. Let's make the most of the time we've got."

Normally, I'd be all over that, but at the moment I'm a little distracted, still smarting from the conversation Logan and I had after school.

He walked out of class at the end of the day, ignoring everyone like usual, but I caught up to him anyway.

"Why did you pretend you didn't know what I was talking about back there?" I ask, still confused by the way he reacted when I asked him about Sadie. "You know Sadie's a half-breed, so why are you..."

Faster than I can react, he spins around and has his hand around my neck. "What did you just call her?"

I choke out my reply. "She's half-human, her father..."

He drops his hand but gives me a disbelieving look. "You don't really believe that crap, do you? That it makes someone any less of a wolf to have a human parent?"

What the hell is he talking about? Of *course* it makes her less. She is *literally* half a wolf. That's what being half-human means.

That's what my father always told me: half-breeds are weaker and a drain on the pack.

I try to explain this to Logan. "My dad says..."

"Your dad's full of shit," he growls back. "You should know that by now."

"You can't talk about him like that!" I know I shouldn't yell at my future Alpha, but I don't know where the hell this is coming from. "He's our Beta and he..."

"...is an ignorant, arrogant prick," Logan finishes, his eyes hard and cold as he glares at me. "And you're going to be just like him if you're not careful. Sadie's no different from you and me, Micah. The sooner you figure that out, the better."

He turns and walks away without another word, leaving me more confused than I've been in a very long time.

And now Blair's trying to get her hands down the front of my jeans, bringing my mind back to the present. "Don't you want me, baby?" she purrs at me as she pulls down my fly. "Are you hard for me yet?"

Blair and I have been sleeping together for a few months now. Everyone at school says we're dating, but that's not really what this is. We just give each other a little stress relief when we need it, and right now I'm more in need of it than ever. Apparently, so is she.

I grab her hair and yank her head back hard, just how she likes it. "You want my cock?" I ask and she nods hungrily. "Then beg for it."

It turns her on to be talked to like this, so I play along for her sake. I'd be happy to just skip straight to the fucking, but she likes a bit of rough foreplay first.

"Please let me have your cock," she whimpers as my fist tightens in her hair. "Fill me up and fuck me hard, please."

That's good enough. I spin her around and bend her over on the kitchen table, lifting the short skirt she's wearing and pulling down her panties just far enough to slide my cock in. She's already wet, of course. She always is.

As I thrust into her hard, Blair cries out my name but my mind is wandering again. I keep my hand on the back of her head, keeping her face down as I drive into her over and over again. When I can't see her face, I can pretend she's anyone at all, and for some reason, today, it's Sadie's face that comes to mind.

I see the way she looked at me this morning in front of the school when she called me an asshole. The defiant look in her eyes makes my cock throbs even harder.

That can't be right. I don't *want* her. She's not even one of us, she's just a half-breed. I try to tell myself the words I've heard my father say so many times, but for some reason it only turns me on more.

Blair's still moaning my name but when I come, it's Sadie's face I see in the blinding light behind my eyelids.

What the hell is wrong with me?

~~**Aaron's PoV**~~

"Did something happen at school today?"

My mom corners me and Ava as soon as Sadie goes upstairs after school. Sadie told us she was tired and wanted to be alone for a while, and I took that at face value, but my mom seems to think there's some kind of hidden meaning behind it.

"I think she's honestly just tired," I tell my mom. "It's kind of draining meeting new people."

It is for me at least, but I don't think my mom and Ava understand. They're both extroverts who thrive on being around other people.

"I don't think anything happened," Ava adds, grabbing a freshly-baked cookie off the tray our mom has just pulled out of the oven. "But there were a few times when people almost blew it. You better tell Sadie the truth soon or she's going to find out all on her own."

Our mom frowns. "I know. I just don't want to overwhelm her, she's already going through so much. Maybe tomorrow will be a better day for her."

Personally I don't think it's going to make much difference which day she gets told, it's going to be a shock to her no matter what.

"Aaron, can you stick around for a while?" Mom asks. "Ava and I need to go run some errands, but I don't want to leave the house empty in case Sadie comes down."

That's fine with me. "Laurel was just going to come over and do some studying anyway. Is that okay?"

My mom's kind of old-fashioned about me and Laurel hanging out alone together even though we've been dating for so long.

"That's fine, just stay downstairs."

The message is loud and clear: no hanging out in my bedroom.

My mom really doesn't need to worry though. Laurel and I might make out, but we rarely go any farther. We definitely haven't slept together. Laurel wants to wait until we both have our wolves and we know we're mates. She figures that will make it even more special.

And it's only a few days away now. My birthday is Saturday and Laurel already has her wolf, so as soon as we see each other at my party, we'll know for sure. I really don't have any doubts though. I'd loved Laurel since pretty much the first day we met, and I know she's my mate.

I've asked her if her wolf acts any differently around me, but she says it's too early, that we won't know for sure until her wolf calls to mine, once I have him.

I really can't wait.

Laurel arrives just as Mom and Ava are heading out and soon, we settle at the kitchen table to go over our history homework together.

"Did you know that Logan walked Sadie to class this afternoon?" she asks out of the blue as we're reading about the last great werewolf war.

"Where did you hear that?"

"I saw it," she explains. "They came into Chemistry together. Everyone was shocked."

I can imagine. It's been a long time since Logan paid attention to anybody. He's been in his own world for a long time now.

"He's probably being nice because she's new."

"Maybe." Laurel doesn't sound convinced. "But we had that other new boy earlier this year and he didn't pay any attention."

That's true. "Maybe he can relate to her losing her parents," I suggest instead.

Laurel nods. "Yeah, that makes sense. It would be good if they could be friends. Maybe he'll be more like himself. I miss Logan."

I do too. We all do. He used to be the most popular guy in school, the one everyone wanted to be around, and one of my best friends. Now, he's just completely closed off and no one knows how to break through.

"So, have you decided what you're wearing to my party?" I ask her, changing the subject. I've been fantasizing about what Laurel will look like the moment we know we're mates.

She gives me a teasing grin, totally onto me. "You're going to have to wait and see."

Her smile fades a bit as she looks down at her hands.

"Aaron, have you thought about what will happen if we're not mates?"

My heart skips a beat. "Don't even say that, Laurel. You know we are."

"I hope we are," she says, which isn't at all the same thing as knowing it.

"Laurel." I say her name firmly, making her look up at me. "You're my mate. Don't ever doubt it."

"I don't want to doubt," she says, her eyes still looking unsure. "But my wolf is being weird when I try to ask her about it."

That makes my stomach sink. "Weird how?"

"I can't really explain. It's like she's talking in riddles."

For the first time, I really let myself imagine that Laurel's not my mate, but I can't do it for long. It feels so wrong, I have to shut it down.

"My wolf will set her straight," I say firmly, even though I haven't even met him yet.

That makes Laurel smile, at least. "If he's as persuasive as you, you might be right."

She leans forward to kiss me, but before our lips connect, I notice someone standing at the door.

"Sadie?"

Fuck. How much of that did she just hear?

Chapter Three

~~Sadie's PoV~~

I tried to sleep for a little while, but there are too many thoughts in my head, so eventually, I get up and go downstairs to get a glass of water. I hear voices as I get closer to the kitchen and realize it's Aaron and Laurel. I don't want to interrupt them if they're having a date or something, so I stop just outside the door to try to see what they're talking about, but their conversation makes absolutely no sense.

They keep mentioning wolves talking to them. Is that some kind of slang here that I don't know?

Aaron sees me right as I step inside. "Sadie?"

He looks nervous, like he's been caught doing something wrong. Laurel quickly leans back and I realize they must have just been about to kiss. *Oops.*

"Sorry, I didn't mean to interrupt. I just wanted to grab some water."

I head to the sink as Aaron and Laurel exchange glances. They still look a bit nervous.

"Do you want to join us?" Laurel offers. "We're just finishing up this homework and we could just watch some TV or whatever."

"Nah, you guys don't need a third wheel around," I tell them, giving them as good a smile as I can. "I'm just going to head back upstairs."

I turn to go, but Aaron stops me. "Did you, uh... did you hear what we were just talking about?"

So, it *was* something I wasn't supposed to hear. I wonder what 'wolf' is code for. Some kind of drugs? That doesn't seem likely. Aaron is too squeaky clean for that. I have no idea what else it could be though.

He looks worried, so I lie. "No, I didn't hear anything. Why? You're not planning a surprise for me, are you?"

He lets out a relieved breath. "No, you don't need to worry about that. I'll let you know when Mom's back and supper's ready."

"Thanks."

I head back upstairs, still curious. I wonder if I can find a way to ask Ava about it without getting Aaron in trouble.

After supper, Ava asks if I want to go out for a walk. I really just want to go back to bed, but I know she's trying to make me feel better, so I agree. We head out into the town and I think again just how clean and perfect-looking this town is. It's nothing like the city where I lived with my mom and dad. There don't seem to be any homeless people here or any rundown houses.

And everyone is really, really good-looking. Even the older people we pass on the streets who say hi to us politely are all good-looking for their age. Maybe there's something in the water.

Ava chats away about school and her upcoming birthday party, not seeming to need much of an answer from me, which is good since I don't feel much like talking. I do take the opportunity to ask her my question though when she stops for a second to take a breath.

"I overheard someone earlier talking about a wolf. Do you know what that means?"

Ava's eyes go wide. "What were they saying?"

I try not to reveal too much, so she doesn't know it's her brother I'm talking about. "Just something about a wolf talking to them. And something about mates?"

Ava clenches her jaw. "That's weird. I don't know what that would mean. Must have been some kind of game they were playing or something."

She's lying to me, I know she is. But why? What doesn't she want me to know?

Then her face goes even stonier, and I turn to see what she's looking at. I feel my face going hard too when I see who's walking up to us.

"Hey, Ava," Micah says, acting like I'm not even there. "I'm surprised to see you out."

He doesn't say it, but I know what he means. He's surprised to see her out with *me*.

"It's a free country, Micah," Ava snaps back at him. "We can go for a walk."

"And what're you going to do if there's an attack?" he asks, giving her a smug smirk. "How will you explain that to your little mutt?"

I have no idea what he's talking about, but he's called me a mutt one too many times. "What the hell is your problem?" I explode, taking a step towards him.

He looks at me in surprise, like he wasn't expecting me to say anything, and for a moment, I think I see admiration in his eyes. It quickly disappears though, and I'm sure I must have imagined it, so I keep talking.

"You don't know anything about me, so you've got no right to act like you're better than me."

"I *am* better than you," he snarls back at me, only anger on his face now. "So is everyone else here, they're just too polite to say it."

"Well, I'm not too polite to kick your ass if you don't leave me alone," I threaten him, but it only makes him laugh.

"I'd like to see you try." He gives me a derisive look before turning back to Ava. "Better keep her on a leash if you don't want her to get bitten."

He walks off and I almost start after him, but Ava holds me back. "Let him go, Sadie. He's not worth it. Sorry he's such a jerk, he's not usually like that. Or at least not quite that bad."

"I'm just lucky then?" I say sarcastically, and she laughs.

"I guess so. Come on though, Micah's right about one thing. It's time we should head back inside."

~~**Logan's PoV**~~

The sun streams in through my bedroom window, warming my face as I start to wake up, and for a moment, I smile. I must have been having some kind of pleasant dream, though I can't remember what it was now. I just know that I felt strong and happy and useful.

But as my eyes open, reality comes rushing back in. Maybe that was the person I used to be, but it's not anymore. Ever since I let down the people who were relying on me the most, nothing in my life seems right.

Just as that familiar feeling of dread starts to settle in, another face flashes in front of my eyes, and immediately my spirits rise a little bit.

It's Sadie's face, but I don't know why it should appear to me at all. Why do I keep thinking about her?

At first, I thought it was just because her parents had died and I could relate to what she was going through. But after my argument with Micah yesterday, when I got home and did my training in the gym, my thoughts kept going back to her again, thinking about what a big shock it's going to be for her to find out she's a werewolf. I'm worried about her and how she'll react. Maybe I should talk to Ava or Aaron and find out what's going on with that, when she's going to be told and how. She's been through enough already. If there's anything I can do to soften the blow, I want to help.

I almost laugh at myself as the thought crosses my mind. When's the last time I really talked to anybody or tried to help them? For the last year, I've been living in a bubble, part of the world but separate from it too, and now, suddenly, I find I'm wanting to step outside the shell I made for myself and pay attention to someone else.

What is it about this girl that's gotten to me?

Whatever it is, there's no time to figure it out now. After throwing some clothes on, I head downstairs to the Alpha's private dining room. The packhouse has a big dining room that's used by everyone who lives and works in the house, but I haven't eaten in there for the last year and neither has my dad. He's in our small dining room when I go in and he nods his head to me in greeting.

"Busy day, Logan?"

He always asks me that, though he knows as well as I do that I'll be going to school and then coming home to train in private just like I have every day for the last year. If there's no school, I just stay home and train. It never changes.

He never says anything to me about it either. He's coping in his own way, so he leaves me to deal with it in mine.

We never mention the two empty seats at the small dining table.

"The usual," I answer him, grabbing some toast and eggs that the staff have already left for us in the middle of the table. "You?"

Normally, he'll give me the same short answer, but today, he pauses. "We got another report last night from the Northaven Pack. The same sort of thing that happened in Moon Valley last week happened there too."

I look up at him in surprise. He told me about Moon Valley a couple of days ago and we both thought it must have been a random event. But if it's happening elsewhere too, maybe there's more to it.

"What could be causing it?" I ask, feeling confused. I've never heard of anything like this happening at all, let alone twice in one week, in two different packs.

"I don't know," my dad admits. "But something strange is going on. I'm going to talk to the Northaven Alpha today and see what else I can find out. Do you want to join me?"

He's been trying to involve me more in pack business as my 18th birthday approaches, and normally, I'd jump at a chance to get out of school. But today, I picture Sadie looking at my empty desk in math class, wondering where I am, and I hesitate.

I'm being stupid, I know. She probably wouldn't even notice if I'm not there, but I feel like I want to be there to help her in case she needs it.

I want to protect her, even though I haven't felt capable of protecting anyone for a long time. It scares me a little, but not necessarily in a bad way.

"I've got a test I shouldn't miss," I lie to my dad, not wanting to try to explain to him the real reason I'd rather go to school. "But I'll come see you after and find out what he said."

My dad nods in agreement. "Okay. Have a good day then, Logan."

"You too, Dad."

I shove the last bit of toast in my mouth as I get up and walk out the door.

~~Ava's PoV~~

I do my best to usher Sadie into school the next morning without running into Micah again. I don't know exactly what his problem is, but if anyone's going to blow the secret before my mom talks to Sadie, it's going to be him, so it's better if we just stay away from him entirely.

I walk Sadie to her homeroom and then go across the hall into mine. My crush, Jordan, is in my homeroom too, and he smiles and says hi to me as I come in, which makes my stomach flutter. But immediately afterwards, he turns back to his conversation with Adam like I'm not even there. With a sigh, I drop into my desk.

Just a few more days, I remind myself. It'll be my birthday and I can find out who my mate is, assuming he's in our pack at all. Maybe he's not. Maybe he's even human, like Sadie's dad. It's impossible to guess what the moon goddess has planned, but I offer up a silent prayer anyway, asking her to at least think about making Jordan my mate if she hasn't already decided who it will be.

The morning goes quickly and soon, we're all back in the cafeteria for lunch. Sadie has a scowl on her face when she comes in, and I rush up to her. "What's wrong?"

"What are the rules on violence at this school?" she asks in reply, not answering my question. "How much trouble am I going to get in if I sucker punch someone?"

"Someone named Micah?" I guess. I know he's in her homeroom, but I hoped he'd behave during class at least.

"No one in particular. Just hypothetically," she says, smiling a little to tell me that it's not hypothetical at all.

"Trust me, there are way more fun ways to get in trouble than wasting your energy on Micah," I assure her. "Let's go grab some lunch."

We get our food and head to our table to sit down, but as we get close, my steps slow in shock.

Logan is sitting at our table.

He's looking at his phone, like usual, but he's actually sitting with us, not on his own like he has every other day this year. I shoot Aaron a look that says 'what the hell?' and he just shrugs back at me, as confused as I am.

Does it have something to do with Sadie? It's the only thing I can think of that's different about today from every other day this year.

I'm just about to suggest to Sadie that she take the seat next to Logan when suddenly Micah swoops in out of nowhere and drops into that seat.

"Hey, Logan," he says, ignoring the rest of us as Sadie and I sit down on the other side of the table instead.

Logan looks up from his phone and his eyes sweep the table, resting on Sadie for just a second longer than everyone else before he turns back to Micah. "Hey."

It's just one word, but the rest of us are stunned into silence. Logan's actually interacting with us? This is so weird.

"My dad said the Alpha's going to Northaven today," Micah says, eagerly jumping on the opening Logan's given him. "What's going on over there?"

Everyone else is quiet, waiting for Logan's reply, but Sadie leans over and whispers to me. "What's an Alpha?"

Although it was a whisper, Logan clearly hears it because he glances over at Sadie for a second before turning back to Micah with a frown. "You really can't follow one simple instruction?"

Micah gives him a confused look. "What instruction?"

Logan sighs in frustration. "Never mind."

He stands up from the table like he's going to leave, but a loud siren rings out and everyone in the cafeteria suddenly goes completely still.

Sadie looks over at me in confusion. "What is that? Fire alarm?"

"Not exactly," I mumble, looking to Aaron for help. What am I supposed to tell her?

The alarm means another pack's wolves have entered our territory. The adult wolves all get alerted through mind-link, but for the school, they use the siren. We all know what to do: we're supposed to go back to our homerooms and the teachers will lock down the school and shift to protect us.

Micah's words when we ran into him last night come back to me: *What're you going to do if there's an attack?* I glance at him, wondering if he did this somehow just to mess with Sadie, but I quickly dismiss the thought. Not even he would be that petty. You don't mess around with things like this.

"Everybody move!" Logan's voice suddenly rings out across the cafeteria and everyone who had been frozen in place springs into action at the authority in his voice. His eyes are full of concern as he looks over at me and Sadie. "Ava, take Sadie to the principal's office. I'll make sure everyone else gets where they need to be."

It's the first time I've seen even a glimpse of the old Logan in so long, I'm stunned into silence. When I don't answer, he narrows his eyes at me.

"What are you waiting for?"

"Sorry, sir," I reply, deferring to him as I'm trained to do in moments like this.

I take Sadie's arm and pull her through the busy halls, everyone returning to their homerooms, doors being slammed and locked behind them.

There's no one in the principal's office when we get there, as Logan must have realized. The principal and other admin staff will be out patrolling the perimeter, protecting the students, in their wolf forms.

We go into the empty office and I close and lock the door behind us.

"What's going on, Ava?" Sadie asks, sounding nervous. I can't imagine what she's thinking.

I scramble for the nearest equivalent thing I can think of from the human world. "There might be an active shooter," I say. "We're locking down."

Understanding immediately crosses over Sadie's face, along with a twinge of fear. "Oh. I guess I didn't expect that here, Westbridge seems so safe."

"It usually is," I try to reassure her. "Hopefully it's just a false alarm."

Sadie looks around the empty room. "Why did we come in here? Where did everyone else go?"

That's a harder question to answer, but I do the best I can. "You haven't done the lockdown drills yet, so Logan probably thought it was safer for us to come here."

Sadie nods, but another look of confusion clouds her face. "Why did you call him 'sir'?"

I wish I didn't have to keep lying, but it's too late to turn back now. "He's kind of in charge when this sort of thing happens. Let's just get down behind the desk here and keep quiet, okay?"

She nods again and we both go and sit behind the principal's desk, waiting for the all-clear signal.

For a while, all we hear is the ticking of the clock, marking the seconds as they go by, but then another sound reaches my ears, and my blood immediately runs cold.

"Ava?" Sadie whispers nervously to me. "Do you hear that?"

I nod, unable to meet her eye, as I bring my finger to my lips, giving her the signal to stay quiet.

Then we hear it again, louder and right outside the door.

The unmistakable growl of a wolf.

Chapter Four

~~Sadie's PoV~~

There's some kind of wild animal right outside the door!

Ava looks a little worried, but not nearly as freaked out as she should be. Not nearly as freaked out as I am. My heart pounds frantically in my chest as I try to figure out what the hell is going on.

I don't know what kind of animal it is, but it sounds big and mean and hungry. Maybe a bear? Do they have bears here? How did it get in the school? What does it have to do with the shooter?

I'm so confused, but when I open my mouth to ask Ava another question, she just shakes her head at me quickly, putting her finger back to her lips again, telling me to keep quiet so I immediately shut my mouth again. As many questions as I have, I don't want to let the animal know that we're here.

After a moment, the growling stops and then someone... or some*thing*... tries to turn the door knob, and I can't help it: I let out a small shriek. This is like some kind of horror movie. It can't really be happening, can it? How could an animal try to open the door?

We hear shouts from further away and the door knob stops moving. A few seconds later, the growling is back. There are more growls and other sounds, like a roar or a howl, and the sound of things... or maybe bodies... being thrown around in the hallway.

I keep waiting for gunshots, but they don't come. There are only the strange noises, like animals fighting, until finally, it goes quiet.

"Is it over?" I whisper to Ava as quietly as I can.

"I'm not sure," she whispers back.

We sit there quietly for a while longer until we hear three short beeps followed by three longer ones, and Ava breathes a sigh of relief.

"That's the all clear," she explains in her regular voice as she gets to her feet, holding out her hand to pull me up too. "It's over now."

That's good news, but I still have no idea what 'it' was. What the hell just happened?

Ava opens the door to the hallway and there are a bunch of men standing around, adult men, talking to each other, and all wearing nothing but loose shorts.

Where on earth did they come from? And why are they half naked?

Ava tries to close the door again when she sees them, but she's not quick enough. One of them spots us and calls out. "Who's in there?"

Ava grimaces before opening the door again. "It's Ava Miller, Beta. I have my cousin Sadie with me."

The man looks at us both in disapproval. "What were you doing in there? That's not the standard protocol."

"No, sir," Ava agrees. "But Logan told me to bring Sadie here. She's the new girl who's just moved to town."

She says 'the new girl' in kind of a funny way, like it means something else besides what she's saying, and his eyes immediately move to me with a hard, condescending expression.

"I see," he says in a clipped voice, sounding not so different from Micah and the way he talks to me. "The human one. Get her out of here, Ms Miller."

"Yes, sir," Ava replies meekly, taking me by the arm and pulling me down the hallway.

Once we're on our own, I pull my arm away from her and turn to face her. "Okay, what the hell is going on here, Ava?"

She gives me a sheepish, nervous look. "What do you mean?"

"Don't treat me like an idiot!" I say, my voice getting louder as I start to get angrier. She's lying to me, just like before, and I'm tired of it. "There's something strange going on in this town. Ever since I got here, people have been acting weird around me. And now this! What kind of animal was that outside the door? Why did that man just call me 'the human one'? What the hell is going on?!"

Ava swallows hard, looking miserable, but before she can answer me, another voice speaks up from behind me.

"Maybe I can explain."

~~Micah's PoV~~

As soon as I offer to answer Sadie's questions, Ava scowls at me. "We don't need any help from you, Micah."

In spite of that, Sadie turns around and eyes me curiously. "Wait. I want to hear what he has to say."

That surprises me. She's been fighting with me all day... okay, to be fair, only after I told her off first... and now, she suddenly wants to hear me out? She must really be desperate for answers.

And I think she should have them too. Maybe then she'll realize why she isn't the same as us, and why she shouldn't give me that look, the one that says that *I'm* not good enough for *her*.

The look that makes me want to slap her and kiss her at the same time.

I open my mouth to answer her, ignoring Ava's frantic head shaking and arm waving, but before I can get any words out, I hear my name being called from down the hall.

"Micah, come here."

It's my dad, so I have to obey, and I give Sadie a shrug. "Sorry. I guess it'll have to wait. But come find me after school if you really want to know the truth."

The idea of seeing Sadie alone after school gets me way more excited than it should. I try to think about unsexy things as I walk over to where my dad and the rest of his team are waiting so they don't notice the bulge in my pants.

"What's going on?" I ask as I walk up to the group. "Who attacked us?"

My dad gestures with his head to one of the classrooms and I peer through the window in the door. There's a man in there, naked and restrained. He must be the wolf that I heard, but why anyone would want to attack the school is a total mystery to me. There's nothing valuable here.

"He's not talking," my dad says. "Yet."

His mouth twists upward into a grim smile and I know he's thinking about all the ways he might make him talk. My dad is good at a lot of things, but breaking people is his favorite. He's shown me some of the tools he uses, and to be honest, they made me feel a little sick. Not that I could tell him that, of course. I pretended I thought it was just as cool as he does.

I've got no problem with ripping a wolf's throat out if it's coming at me in a fight, but pulling a guy's claws out when he's tied up? Not really the same thing.

I'd never say that to my dad, of course. I don't want him thinking I'm weak.

"What do you need from me?" I ask. There must be a reason he called me over.

"What do you know about that half-breed girl?" he asks, giving a little sneer as he points down the hall to where Sadie was. I turn to look for her, but she and Ava are gone, and my heart beats a little faster. He doesn't suspect anything about the weird things I've been thinking about her, does he? How could he?

"Not much," I say, trying to sound casual. "She's the Millers' cousin, her parents died, she doesn't know she's a wolf. Just the same things we were all told at the assembly." He nods, and I can't help asking: "Why?"

My dad looks back at the tied-up wolf. "He was trying to get in the room where she and the Miller girl were hiding. I don't know if it was on purpose. I'll find out from him, but I just thought I'd see if you knew anything that might be special about her."

Special? Sadie's face flashes in front of me again, her dark chocolate eyes and her dark hair framing her oval face.

That sexy look of defiance on her face.

For fuck's sake, I'm getting hard again.

"Not that I've seen," I answer before trying to change the subject. "Do you think it's got anything to do with what's going on at the other packs?"

Disapproval fills his eyes. "What would it have to do with that?"

My cheeks start to color in response. I hate when he talks to me like I'm an idiot. "I don't know exactly, I just thought since they're happening at the same time..."

"Lots of things happen at the same time, Micah." His voice is cold and mocking, and I can't bring myself to look at the other warriors. Why can't he ever, just once, say I might have a point?

"I'm sorry, sir."

He nods curtly. "You're dismissed. Get back to class."

I grumble as I make my way back down the hall. He never takes what I say seriously. He treats me like a fucking child still, but I'm 18, I've got my own wolf, and I should be part of his team, defending the pack and investigating the attacks, getting ready to take over as Beta, not stuck in some stupid class learning stuff I'll never use.

My Geography class goes very slowly but finally, it's time for the last class of the day, which is Chemistry. I walk quicker than usual to get there, and I only realize when I get to the door that it's because I know Sadie's in the class too. When I look around, though, she's not there yet. My other classmates shuffle in, one by one or in pairs, until there are only two empty seats left.

Sadie's and Logan's.

Logan isn't a huge surprise, he often misses class for no reason, and after that attack earlier, he's probably got stuff to do. I bet my dad doesn't make fun of him if *he* makes a suggestion.

But that's not what's really bothering me right now. Where's Sadie? Did Ava end up telling her the truth?

And does that mean she won't be coming to see me after school after all?

I'm way more disappointed about that than I should be. Scowling, I look up at the clock. Another fucking hour to go. This day can't be over soon enough.

~~Sadie's PoV~~

As Micah walks away, I spin back to Ava. "Well?"

If Micah's not going to tell me, then Ava's going to have to.

She pulls another face. "When we get home, we'll talk to my mom, ok? I promise she'll answer all your questions."

Not good enough. I'm tired of being put off, so I turn and start walking towards the exit, but Ava calls after me.

"Wait, you can't go outside, Sadie. It might not be safe yet."

My frustration boils over. "Why the hell not?! Give me a straight answer, Ava, or I'm walking out of here right now."

She grimaces again and hesitates, and that's it. I head for the door. As I push it open, a rush of cold wind hits me, making me shiver. I forgot it's still winter and I left my coat in the classroom. Too late, though, I'm not going back. I rush out into the chilly air anyway and head down the steps, looking from left to right when I reach the street.

I still don't really know my way around this town, but I think there's a park to the right, somewhere it will be quiet with no one else around, so I head that way with my hands shoved in my pocket to keep them warm.

I find the park and as I hoped, there's no one else around, so I sink down onto one of the empty benches, looking down at the ground as all my thoughts race around my head. Why won't anyone just tell me what's going on? There was no shooter today, I'm sure of it, but there was *something* in that school, and something tells me it's not the first time it's happened.

Suddenly, I remember last night and what I overheard between Aaron and Laurel.

They were talking about wolves! Was the thing in the school a wolf? Why are there wild wolves running around the town? It doesn't make any sense, but it's the first connection I've made between all the strange things so I cling onto it.

The wind hits me again, right as a voice speaks up from behind me, making me nearly jump out of my skin.

"You doing okay?"

The voice is strong and deep and immediately, I feel a bit warmer as I turn around to see Logan standing there.

"How did you find me?" I haven't seen him since the cafeteria. Was he looking for me, or did he just randomly come here too?

He gives a casual shrug. "I'm good at tracking. Mind if I sit down?"

I shuffle over on the bench a bit to make more room for him and he comes around to sit beside me. I shiver again, not just from the cold, and he frowns as he sees me do it.

"Where's your coat?"

I shrug. "I was in a hurry, I didn't grab it."

Without asking, he pulls the zipper of his coat down and shrugs it off before handing it to me. "Here."

I want to take it, but I feel bad too. "What about you?"

One corner of his mouth goes up, just a little. "I'll be fine."

I'm too cold to argue so I take the coat from him and slip it over my shoulders. It's warm, not just because of the material but because he was just wearing it. Some of his body heat lingers. It smells good, too, like fresh pine needles, and I try not to inhale too deeply.

That would just look weird.

"What brings you out here?" he asks, gesturing to the empty park.

I answer his question with one of my own. "What just happened in the school?"

It's a challenge. I want to know if he'll tell me the truth or if he'll lie to me like everyone else.

But to his credit, he replies straight away. "There was an intruder. I don't know all the details yet, but someone broke in, looking for something. He's been captured and they'll be questioning him soon."

He? But what about the animal I heard?

I decide to ask. "Did he bring some kind of animal with him? I heard growling."

Logan nods. "Yeah. He had a wolf with him."

Well, that's something. I'm not going totally crazy then.

"Who has a pet wolf?" I can't help asking.

Logan smiles again, just that small, barely-there smile, almost like his mouth has forgotten how to do it but is trying to remember. "Actually, it's pretty common around here."

I think back to what I heard Aaron and Laurel discussing, about talking to wolves. "Why?"

Logan takes a breath before looking me straight in the eye. His eyes are a rather startling shade of green, and this close up, they're nearly mesmerizing. "I don't know if you should hear this from me, but in some ways, maybe it's better that it's someone you don't really know. At least you know I've got no reason to lie to you."

I frown as I try to make sense of what he's saying. "Lie to me about what?"

"About what we are. Me and everyone else in this town. There's something different about us than the people you used to live with, Sadie."

"Tell me something I don't know," I grumble, and again, he almost smiles.

"I'm trying to. You've heard about supernatural creatures, right? Vampires, mermaids, demons, that sort of thing?"

My frown gets deeper. What the hell does this have to do with anything? "Sure. I read books."

He nods. "Well, those writers didn't completely make everything up. They get a lot of stuff wrong, but those species all really exist, and there are other ones too."

He's got to be kidding me. Is this some kind of prank on the new girl? It must be, but as I look into his green eyes, there's no hint of a joke. He looks completely serious.

"There's a whole species known as shifters. They look like humans for the most part, but they can change their form into different animals. There are dragons, lions, bears, anything big and scary you might think of. And wolves too."

We were back to wolves. "You mean like werewolves?" I ask, trying to follow his train of thought.

His face brightens a little. "Yeah, exactly. What do you know about werewolves?"

I try to think. "I mean, I've seen Twilight. But that's about it."

He winces.

"That fucking movie..." he mutters under his breath before shaking his head. "Okay, forget everything you know, then. But Sadie, what I need to tell you is that werewolves are real. The animal you heard in the school was a wolf, but it was also a man, a man who was in his wolf form. He can change back and forth between the two. And so can just about everyone in this town."

My mind blanks as I try to take in what he's saying. It has to be some kind of joke. This makes no sense at all.

"We're all werewolves," he says, looking somehow apologetic and proud at the same time. "Including me."

Is he crazy? Just when I thought I had met someone really interesting, he has to go and turn out to be insane?

And then he says something even crazier.

"Most importantly, Sadie, you're one too."

Chapter Five

~~Logan's PoV~~

After I tell Sadie she's a werewolf, she just stares at me blankly, not blinking, and I start to get a bit worried. Was that too much? Maybe I should have eased into it a bit more, but I thought it might be better to just rip the band-aid right off and tell her the whole truth. It might be shocking at first but it was better to know.

Gradually, her blank look turns to disbelief. "Are you high?" she asks, a look of concern on her face.

Again, I almost laugh. It's weird how often that happens when I'm with her. "No, Sadie, I'm definitely not high. I know it might be difficult to accept at first, but it's true. Your mom was a shifter, and you are too."

She shakes her head, definitely not believing me. "I can guarantee I have never turned into a wolf before."

"Of course not," I quickly agree. "You won't get your wolf until you're 18. That's not for a few weeks yet, right?"

I don't know why I remember that. It was mentioned at the assembly when they told us about Sadie, but there's no reason it should have stuck in my head.

"But you can turn into a wolf?" she challenges me, smirking a little. "Okay, then. Show me."

My lips tighten as I anticipate her reaction to my answer. "I'm not 18 yet either. I will be at the end of the month, and that's when I'll get my wolf."

"So I'm supposed to believe you just because you say so?" she asks, shaking her head again. Obviously, she doesn't believe me at all. "I don't know what kind of joke this is, Logan, but I don't like it."

"It's not a joke," I promise her, frowning as she starts to stand up. I take hold of her arm to stop her. "Sadie, wait. I can prove it to you. Just come with me to the pack house."

Her brow furrows at that. "Pack house? What's that?"

"Werewolves live in packs," I explain. "Westbridge might look like just a regular town, but everyone here is a member of the same wolf pack. The pack house is the main building for all the pack business, and it's where the Alpha lives."

"Alpha?" she repeats curiously, and I know she's remembering that Micah mentioned the Alpha in the cafeteria either. Maybe that will help her to believe me, so I latch onto that.

"That's right. The Alpha is the head of the pack, the one in charge. Everyone listens to him or her. In our pack, it's a man." I don't mention yet that he's my father. I figure I'll let her get used to the whole idea first.

"So, you want me to go with you to some random house?" She sounds unimpressed. "I grew up in a city, Logan. My parents taught me not to go home with strangers."

The words are out of her mouth before she even thinks them through, and I see the moment she realizes what she's said and how the mention of her parents makes her wince in pain. It's a pain I know all too well.

"Then let me walk you home," I offer instead, not wanting to cause her any more stress. "You can talk to your aunt and she'll explain everything."

Sadie looks a bit uncertain. "You want me to tell my aunt what you told me?"

I nod. "Yeah, she can prove to you that it's true. She'll shift for you if you want. She's a werewolf too, Sadie. Like I said, we all are."

I can tell she still doesn't believe me, but she's a bit thrown off by my suggestion that her aunt will back me up.

We both get up and start to walk over towards the Millers' house.

"Okay, let's say I believe you," Sadie says after a couple of minutes of silence. "Which I don't, but for the sake of argument, let's pretend I do. If my parents and I are werewolves and werewolves like in packs, why didn't we live in a pack?"

That's a pretty easy one to answer. "Your mom was a werewolf but your dad wasn't. He was human. I don't know exactly why they chose to live outside the pack, but they did."

I could guess why, but I don't want to get into anti-human prejudice with Sadie right now. She has enough to deal with without bringing that into it.

I also don't know why her parents never told her the truth. Were they planning to before they died? What were they going to do when she turned 18?

"So humans and werewolves can... intermingle?" she asks, looking a bit embarrassed.

I know exactly what she's asking. "They can mate, yeah. When we're in human form, we're just like humans. The DNA's close enough that we can have babies with humans. It's not that common though. Most werewolves are mated to other wolves."

"Mated?" she repeats curiously. "Like married?"

"Kind of." Should I explain to her about mates right now? It's a pretty big subject. Probably better to convince her that werewolves are real first, but I try to explain at least a little bit. "Our wolves recognize their mates, the person that they're meant to be with. It's all planned for us ahead of time by the moon goddess, she pairs wolves up with the partner they're meant to be with."

"So you don't get any say in it?" Sadie asks. Her nose wrinkles in disapproval. "Like an arranged marriage. What if it's someone you hate?"

"You can reject your fated mate," I explain. "But it's usually not necessary. There's a reason mates are chosen, even if it's not obvious right away."

She doesn't say anything else so I stay silent too until we get to her house. Her aunt comes rushing out the front door as we walk up.

"Sadie, are you okay? The school just called and said you left, I was so worried."

Sadie looks between her aunt and me. "Things at school got a little intense. I just had to get some fresh air."

I'm not sure if she's going to tell her aunt what we talked about, so I decide that I will. She needs to talk about this with someone she trusts. "Mrs Miller, I was just telling Sadie about the pack and her place in it, but I think she still has some questions."

Mrs Miller's mouth falls open as she looks at me. She definitely wasn't expecting that, and her eyes move nervously from me to Sadie. "Oh. Well, thank you, Logan. Do you want to come in?"

I kind of do, but I think it's better that they talk in private, so I decline. "No, thanks, I need to go check in with my father. I'll see you at school tomorrow, Sadie."

I turn and walk away, leaving them to what I'm guessing will be a very awkward conversation.

By the time I get back to the pack house, my dad is already back from Northaven. They must have called him back after the infiltration at the school.

"Where have you been?" he asks as I walk into his office. He's not angry, just curious. "I called the school but they said you'd gone."

"Just looking out for someone," I say vaguely. He's got more important things to worry about than Sadie right now. I can take care of her. "What do we know about the guy from the school?"

"Not much," he admits. "Aldric is questioning him now."

Poor bastard. I've never met anyone who can stand up to our Beta's interrogations.

"But it's Northaven I want to talk to you about," my dad continues, pointing at the chair on the other side of the desk. I sit down, waiting for him to explain. "It's pretty much exactly the same thing that Moon Valley reported, except this time it's even more obvious that it's a mistake."

I frown as I try to figure out what that means. The report we had from Moon Valley last week was the first time I'd ever heard of anything like this happening. Two young werewolves, one 19 and one 20, suddenly discovered they were mates. On the surface there was nothing odd about that, except that they had worked together in the same team for more than a year, seen each other every day, and there had never been a hint of them being mates before. Then out of the blue, both of their wolves declared that they were mates after all, even though their human sides had no attraction to each other.

Confused, they'd gone to their Alpha for help, and he in turn had reached out to the other Alphas in the area, including my dad, to see if any of them had heard of this happening before. Nobody had.

Until now, I guess. "What happened in Northaven?"

"A girl turned 18," my dad explains. "And found her mate at her birthday party."

So far, it sounds normal enough. I wait for the catch.

"It was her brother."

I wince. "That's not possible, is it? Unless he's adopted or something?"

"He's not adopted," my dad says. "Neither of them is. They're biologically brother and sister, and no, it's not possible. So I think we have to accept that something very strange is happening. The moon goddess' instructions are getting scrambled somehow, and if we don't figure out how to fix it, we could all end up in a very big mess."

~~Sadie's POV~~

After Logan walks away, my aunt turns to me with a nervous expression. "What did Logan tell you, exactly?"

As soon as she asks me, I realize I'm absolutely exhausted. All the stress of the day hits me all at once and I just want to sit down. "Can we go inside?"

"Of course." She looks embarrassed that she didn't suggest it first. "Come on, I'll get you some milk and cookies."

That almost makes me smile. Are milk and cookies supposed to make me feel better? Maybe that worked when I was 5 and skinned my knee, but I've got bigger problems now.

Still, I follow her into the kitchen and sit down at the table. She busies herself making up a plate of cookies and pouring the milk before coming and sitting down across from me.

"I'm sorry I didn't tell you myself, Sadie," she says, and I can see she really does feel bad. "I should have told you right away when you got here, I just thought you were already going through enough. I didn't want to overwhelm you."

I try to understand what she's saying. She can't actually mean that Logan was telling me the truth?

"What should you have told me?"

She gives me a sheepish smile. "That you're a werewolf, just like us."

I want to believe she's lying, just like I thought Logan was, but why would she lie to me about this? It doesn't make any sense. "Show me," I demand, just like I did with Logan. "I want to see you turn into a wolf."

I expect her to make up an excuse just like he did, but she doesn't. She just nods solemnly. "Okay, if you want."

She stands up from the table and I keep my eyes glued to her. Is this some kind of magic trick? What is she going to do?

"I'm just going to take my clothes off, honey," she says. "Otherwise they'll get torn when I shift, and I really like this blouse."

This just keeps getting weirder and weirder, but I keep my mouth shut as she takes off her shirt and skirt and places them on the kitchen counter. She leaves her underwear on, at least.

Her body sort of hunches over, and it's like her back is getting longer, but I know that's not possible. I blink, trying to make my eyes work properly, but all I can see is fur starting to grow out of her skin, and almost before I know it, there's a real live wolf in front of me, right where my aunt was standing.

It takes a step towards me and immediately, I shrink back. Just as quickly, it stops moving. My heart is pounding and I almost feel sick. This can't be real. This doesn't happen in real life.

But it *is* happening, right in front of me. I can see it with my own eyes, so, as unlikely as it might seem, I have to accept that it really must be true.

The wolf steps back, behind the island in the kitchen, and a moment later, a hand appears, grabbing the clothes off the counter. In another minute, my aunt reappears, dressed again.

"Sadie?" As she looks at me with concern, I realize my mouth is hanging open. Can she blame me, though? What am I supposed to be feeling right now?

"My mom was a werewolf too?" I manage to whisper, repeating what Logan had told me.

My aunt nods. "Yes. She grew up here in the pack with me and our parents. Then she met your dad, her mate, and they decided to move to the city. You came along a couple of years later."

I look down at my own hands, a million thoughts racing through my head. Will I really be able to do that too? Just turn into a wolf whenever I feel like it? Why would I even want to?

One question is the loudest of all: "Why didn't she tell me?"

A grimace crosses my aunt's face. "She was pretty angry with the pack after the way they treated her mate. Some people didn't accept him because he was human, and you know your mom. She didn't take any crap from anyone."

That's true. My mom always stood up for me whenever anyone tried to knock me down. I always thought of her as some kind of warrior, and maybe she was. A new wave of sadness hits me as I realize how much she never told me about her life, and how many things I'll never get to ask her.

"I'm sure she would have told you soon," my aunt continues. "Since you're going to get your wolf when you turn 18, she would have wanted you to be prepared."

How am I supposed to prepare for something like that?

Finally, something else makes sense to me. "Ava and Aaron are turning 18 this weekend," I say out loud. "That's why they're so excited?"

My aunt nods again, a small smile on her face. "Right. They're both going to get their own wolves, and maybe even find their mates. Did Logan tell you about mates?"

"A little bit." I still think the idea of a pre-destined partner you're supposed to be with is ridiculous, but I'll keep my mouth shut for now. "Do you mind if I go upstairs?"

I have so much to think about, I don't think I can take any more information right now.

"Of course," she says. "Maybe Ava can come up and see you later if you want to talk more."

I agree to that and head up to my room, trying to figure out exactly when my life took such a crazy turn.

~~**Ava's PoV**~~

My mom sends me a text during the last period at school to tell me that Sadie's at home and not to worry. That's a relief. I've been feeling bad that I let her run off, but what was I supposed to do? I couldn't just blurt out the truth to her in the school hallway when she was already upset about the attack.

When I get home, I'm shocked when my mom tells me what happened.

"*Logan* told her?" I repeat, sure that I misheard. What was Logan doing with Sadie?

But my mom nods. "I don't know exactly what he said, but he told her the biggest part, at least, and he brought her home."

I don't know what to make of that, but it's not my biggest concern right now. "How is she?"

"Confused," my mom says sympathetically. "Probably a little scared. Do you want to go talk to her?"

"Of course."

I don't know exactly what I'm going to say, but I head up to Sadie's room anyway. When I knock on the door, a quiet voice tells me to come in, and I open the door to find her sitting on the floor with a framed picture of her parents. She's wearing a coat I don't recognize.

"Hey." I immediately close the door behind me and go to sit down beside her. "How are you doing?"

She looks up from the picture, and although I expect her to look sad or scared, like my mom said, she looks mostly angry instead.

"Why would they lie to me?" she asks me, her voice full of hurt. "My whole life, they kept this a secret. Why?"

I don't know the answer to that. I don't think anyone does, other than her parents themselves, and they're the two people she can never ask.

"I'm sure they thought they were doing the right thing," I say instead. "They wouldn't have done it to hurt you."

She just shakes her head. "Sometimes, when I was little, I used to dream that I was secretly a princess, and someday someone would show up to tell me. I never dreamt anyone would tell me that I'm half-wolf though."

"Hey, being a werewolf is way better than being a princess. What do you get to do as a princess? Wear pretty dresses and go to balls? Well, we can do that too, plus we get to shift and live in the pack and find our mates. It's amazing to be a werewolf, Sadie. You're going to love it!"

I really mean it. I wouldn't want to give up being a werewolf for anything.

"Why is everyone so obsessed with mates?" she wonders, looking back down at the photo. Her fingers glide gently across her dad's face. "I always thought my parents loved each other. But now it turns out they just had to be together because some goddess said so?"

I feel like she's missing the big picture. "Okay, first of all, it's not just 'some goddess', it's the moon goddess who looks after all werewolves like us. And she doesn't make anyone be with someone they don't want to be. She looks at what you need and who you are, and she finds the perfect person for you and then she lets your wolf know so that you can recognize them when you see them. It's amazing, Sadie! Think about humans: they have to date people for so long and then find out that they don't even like each other, and then start all over again? No, thank you. I'll take whatever mate I'm given any day."

I'm not sure she's convinced, but I keep talking anyway.

"And lastly, your parents *did* love each other. Almost all mates do. You still need to get to know your mate and grow to love them, just like anyone. It's just you get to skip that whole part of wondering if they're the right person for you because you already know they are."

She's still silent, looking at the photo, so I move on.

"But that's just part of being a werewolf. We're like a big family, everyone looks out for each other and protects the pack. The Alpha's like a father to all of us."

She finally looks back up at me when I mention the Alpha. "How does this guy get to be in charge of everyone? Is he elected?"

The idea makes me smile. "No. It's hereditary, like a king. His father was Alpha before him, and his son will be Alpha next. It would have been his daughter, since she was born first, but..."

I trail off, realizing I'm getting off topic. There will be time to talk about the rest of the pack later. For now, we should focus on her.

"What other questions do you have?" I ask her. "Consider me your walking werewolf Wikipedia."

That almost gets a smile out of her. "Thanks, Ava. I appreciate it, really, but I think I just want to be alone for a while."

I nod. "Sure. If you change your mind though, you know where to find me."

I get up and go to the door, looking back at her one more time. She's still staring at the picture of her parents and she doesn't look up as I go out and shut the door behind me.

Chapter Six

~~**Micah's PoV**~~

"Hey, baby." Blair slides a hand up my back as the bell rings for the end of class. "My parents are out again for a while tonight. You want to come over?"

Normally I don't have to think about that for a second, but today I hesitate for some reason. Before I can answer, I receive a mind-link from the Alpha.

Micah, Logan would like to see you at the pack house.

That shocks me. Logan hasn't invited me over in a really long time. He can't mind-link me directly yet because he doesn't have his wolf, so his dad must be passing the message on.

I quickly reply: *Yes, sir. I'm on my way.*

"They need me at the pack house," I tell Blair, liking how important it makes me sound. "I don't know how long I'll be, but I'll call you later if I'm free."

I already know I'm not going to call her, though I'm still not really sure why.

I grab my stuff from my locker and head over to the pack house. Normally, as the Beta's family, we'd have our own apartment within the house, but my dad wanted his own space so we live just a couple of houses away. I already think that when I'm Beta, I'll move back into the pack house. This is where the most important people in the pack live. It's where I belong.

"Micah." Logan's voice calls out from down the hall as I start towards the Alpha's office. He's in the smaller room next door, the one that his dad gave him to use. His dad's already treating him like the Alpha he's going to be, unlike my dad who won't even think about delegating anything to me yet.

"Hey," I greet him as I follow him into the room. "What's up?"

Although I try to sound cool, I'm actually really excited that he called me. We haven't talked much over the last year, and though I know it's nothing to do with me specifically, it still hurts. So that's one good thing, and the other is that I'm guessing the reason he called is something to do with the attack, and I want to know what's going on.

We sit down and Logan tells me about the stuff that's going on in the other packs, the crazy, messed up mate matches.

"That's fucked up," I tell him when he tells me about the brother and sister being mates.

He almost smiles. It's the closest I've seen him get to a smile in a long time. "Yeah, just a little bit. Nobody knows what it all means yet, but I thought you should know too."

Pride fills my chest. Maybe my dad doesn't value my opinion, but Logan does. I don't know what's made him come out of himself now and finally be interested in the rest of us again, but I couldn't be happier that it's happening.

There's a knock at the door that connects Logan's little office with the Alpha's much bigger one.

"Yeah?" Logan calls out and the door opens. Ellis, the pack Gamma stands there. He looks a bit surprised to see me, but he addresses himself to both of us.

"Beta Aldric has just finished questioning the wolf we caught earlier. The Alpha wants you to join us."

We both jump to our feet and follow him into the Alpha's office. Alpha Layton gives me a polite nod as I walk in, but my dad doesn't acknowledge me. He speaks directly to the Alpha, ignoring everyone else.

"He didn't know much," he sneers. "But I got everything out of him that he did know."

I was sure he did. I could see traces of blood on his hands if I looked close enough.

"Which was?" the Alpha asks.

"He was sent to kill the half-breed girl."

My heart feels like it stops beating for a second. The guy came here to kill Sadie?

Logan stiffens next to me, but for a different reason, apparently. "She's got a name, Beta. It's Sadie Jennings."

Logan knows her full name? I didn't even know it. Why does he?

My dad isn't impressed with the interruption. "Whatever her name is, she's the reason he was here." He turns back to the Alpha. "But he doesn't know who wants her dead or why. He was hired to do it and it was all anonymous."

Alpha Layton nods, but I can see the pain in his eyes. He must be thinking about what happened last year, the last time someone infiltrated our territory.

"We'll have to look into this," he says, looking around the room. "I don't know enough about this girl to know why she'd be targeted, but obviously, she's a member of our pack now and will be offered our full protection."

His eyes fall on me.

"Micah, I'd like you to provide personal security to her until we get to the bottom of this."

Me? A bunch of different feelings rush through me at once. I'm honored that the Alpha would pick me for an important job like this. I'm a little bit nervous because I've never done anything like it before. And

I'm kind of excited, I have to admit, at the idea of having to spend all my time with Sadie, but I'm confused about why I'm excited.

I really don't know what to feel.

"I can do it," Logan speaks up from beside me, and instantly, my spirits fall. Does he think I can't handle this?

Luckily, the Alpha takes my side. "You don't have your wolf yet. Micah does. If she needs to be defended, he's better able to do that."

I know he doesn't mean it as it sounds, but Logan's face goes pale, and the Alpha instantly hears how it sounded too.

"Logan, I didn't mean…"

Logan doesn't wait for an apology. He storms out of the room, leaving the rest of us in awkward silence.

"Fuck," the Alpha swears under his breath. "I've got to go talk to him. Aldric, you can take the lead on finding out who hired this wolf and why. Micah, you're responsible for Sadie."

"Yes, sir," my dad and I reply in unison and the Alpha hurries out of the room after his son, leaving the rest of us in awkward silence.

Gamma Ellis breaks the silence as he turns to me. "I can give you a briefing on providing personal security, things you should be aware of."

I nod in agreement and glance over at my dad. For a second, I hope maybe he'll say something, like he's proud of me for getting this assignment, or he thinks the Alpha made a good choice. *Any* kind of acknowledgement. But he ignores me, turning to his own team to start making his own plans instead.

I don't know why I even bother sometimes, and I grit my teeth as I turn back to the Gamma. "Let's go."

~~**Sadie's PoV**~~

I walk into the kitchen at breakfast time the next day and immediately, everyone stops talking. Nothing like making me feel like more of an outsider than I already do.

"Good morning, Sadie," my aunt says, standing up and going to the counter. "What would you like for breakfast?"

I'm not really hungry. But I didn't eat supper last night and our lunch yesterday was interrupted by that crazy incident at the school, so I suppose I better eat something.

"Whatever you've got is fine," I tell her. I don't want her going to any extra trouble.

"Hey, Sadie," Aaron greets me as I sit down, looking a little sheepish. "I hear you know all about us now?"

I guess it definitely wasn't a dream. I didn't really think it was, but this just confirms it.

"I know a little," I reply. "I guess there's probably more I still need to learn."

Ava nods enthusiastically, her smile a little too bright. "Like I said, any questions you have, I'm your girl."

My aunt sets a plate of eggs and toast down in front of me. "Are you sure you're up to going to school today, Sadie? I can call in and tell them you need the day off."

It's tempting, but what's the point? It's not going to be any different tomorrow. My parents are still going to be gone and I'm still going to be living in a town of werewolves where I don't understand anything that's happening. I might as well just get used to it.

"It's okay," I say. "I can go."

I eat my breakfast as Ava and Aaron talk about some of their assignments and then almost before I know it we're pulling up outside the school again. I'm barely out of the car when my homeroom teacher Mr Latham appears in front of us. "Good morning Sadie, Ava. Can I speak to you both for a minute?"

Now what? Am I in trouble for cutting out of class yesterday? Maybe, but if that's the case, why is Ava coming along?

We follow Mr Latham into the school and into my homeroom class room. It's empty other than one other person.

Micah.

My eyes narrow at the sight of him, and I expect him to make some sarcastic comment like he always does when he sees me. To my surprise, he just stands there calmly, not saying anything.

"Sit down, please," Mr Latham says to all of us, closing and locking the door behind us. "Now, Sadie, I understand that you now know you're living in a wolf pack."

Word travels fast in this town, apparently. "I do."

"You'll be able to join your classmates in training soon," he continues, and I don't really know what he's talking about but I nod anyway. "But for now, since things are still so new for you, the Alpha has requested that you have someone to look out for you while you're at school. Just in case anything like yesterday happens again."

I don't know which part of that to focus on first. Why do I need someone to look out for me? Is what happened yesterday really that common?

Mr Latham nods towards Micah. "Since you're in several of the same classes already, Micah has volunteered to provide that support for you."

What?

Why would the one person who's been more of a jerk to me than anyone offer to protect me now, unless he thinks he can somehow make my life more miserable? It feels like some kind of trap.

"Mr Latham," Ava speaks up, sounding just as surprised as I am. "Can't Aaron or I do it? We could switch some of our classes around..."

He cuts her off. "There's no need. Mr Geary's already trained and he's already got experience with his wolf, and you won't even get yours until this weekend. Besides, the Alpha's already approved it."

That shuts Ava up. Everyone sure seems to take this Alpha guy seriously.

"I'll leave you to make the arrangements between yourselves," Mr Latham continues. "I trust you can both work together as adults."

He raises an eyebrow at Micah as he says that, so he must have noticed that we don't really get along, and yet, he's sticking me with him anyway.

Mr Latham leaves the room and Ava turns to Micah. "If this is some sort of trick so you can harass Sadie..."

"It's not," he promises, sounding more sincere than I've ever heard him before. "The Alpha gave me a job and I'll do it properly."

That seems to convince Ava. Do I really just have to tell people the Alpha said something and they'll all do whatever I say? That's what it feels like.

Ava turns to me. "Do you want me to stay?"

I'm not sure what good that will do. She and Micah just tend to bicker about me like I'm not even there at times, so I tell her to go ahead and I'll see her at lunch. She leaves the room too, leaving me and Micah alone together.

"So, you know we're all werewolves," he says, repeating what Mr Latham already asked me.

"It looks that way," I answer, still not really willing to say the words out loud. It sounds so crazy.

"And you know what you are?" he continues, a little bit of his usual sneer coming back into his voice.

"The girl who's going to kick your ass if you don't choose your next words very carefully?" I say to him as sweetly as I can.

His face darkens. "I guess you haven't learned everything yet. That's fine, I can explain it to you. We'll have time. For the next little while, Sadie, every time you turn around, I'm going to be there."

Fuck. That's just what I need.

~~**Logan's PoV**~~

As I walk to school in the morning, the conversation I had with my dad yesterday keeps replaying in my head.

During the meeting in his office, I offered to be the one to watch out for Sadie for a few reasons. First, I'm the Alpha's son. The whole pack is going to be my responsibility someday and I already feel responsible for everyone's safety now. Second, Micah is a good fighter and a decent guy, but I know he's got his prejudices when it comes to humans. I've already seen the way he talked to me about Sadie on her first day here.

And third, I just like the idea of hanging out with her. I can't explain it. Maybe it's because she doesn't treat me like everyone else does, like they're walking on eggshells around me. Maybe it's because she knows what it's like to lose someone really close to her. Whatever the case, I like the idea of spending time with her.

But as soon as I suggested it, my dad shot me down, saying that Micah could protect her better than I could, and it felt like all the air rushed out of my body. I couldn't catch my breath. Even though I knew it looked childish, I had to get out of the room. I needed some air, so I ran away.

My dad caught up to me out in the garden at the back of the pack house. I go there a lot when I need to think, so it didn't take him too long to find me.

"I didn't mean that how it sounded, Logan," he apologized. "I wasn't talking about what happened last year."

I knew he wasn't, but how could I not make the connection? When I didn't immediately respond, he took another step towards me.

"It's not your fault, you know. No one blames you."

"They should." My response was quiet but I knew he heard it.

"Why would you think that?" His voice was pained too. We haven't talked about this in so long. We've never really talked about it actually, not fully, but maybe we should. Maybe the time had come to get it all out in the open.

~~One year ago~~

I was just finishing breakfast when we got the alert that someone had entered our territory.

Adrenaline surged through me, but I wasn't afraid. It wasn't like it was the first time it had happened and I had been trained on what to do. Sure, I didn't have my wolf yet, but it didn't matter. My dad would lead the pack warriors out and I would secure the house.

That was my job.

I hurried to the intercom on the wall of the kitchen. "Protocol Six," I announced into the transmitter which would broadcast to all rooms in the pack house. We had different protocols we used in a random rotation, so that if we ever had a traitor in the pack, no one would know ahead of time which one we would use. They wouldn't know where to go to find the people I was in charge of keeping safe.

"Come on, slowpoke!" I looked over at the door to see my sister's smiling face. A year older than me, Kara was going to turn eighteen in just a few days. She couldn't wait to get her wolf and take her place at my father's side to begin her training for the role she was born to inherit.

It was my responsibility to keep her and my mother safe. The Luna and the future Alpha, the pack's most precious assets. I knew what an honor it was to be given this role and I took it very seriously, but I couldn't resist the chance to tease her a bit too.

"You're the slow one, not me," I grinned back at her. "I'll beat you to the basement without breaking a sweat."

Laughing, I shoved past her as she shouted out behind me. "Cheater!"

I could hear her laughter behind me but I didn't stop until we were down at the bottom of the stairs where our mother was already waiting for us, along with all the pack staff who weren't able to fight and the children who lived in the house.

My mom shook her head at me and Kara as we came to a quick halt, me just an arm's length ahead of her. "Can't you two do anything that doesn't turn into a competition?"

There was enough affection in her voice that I knew we weren't really in trouble, so I threw in an extra shot. "It's not really a competition when I keep winning all the time."

Kara smacked the back of my head, and my mom laughed. "You kind of deserved that," she told me. "Now, run through your list."

Right. I needed to focus.

I pulled out my phone that always had an updated list of who should be in the house, and I called off the names quickly to make sure everyone was here. They were, so I ran back up to the top of the stairs and shut the steel door, setting the alarmed lock that would keep any intruders out.

"Everyone into the back room," I commanded and they followed my order immediately. Once inside, I secured that door too for an extra layer of protection. We'd be safe there, I was sure of it. We always had been before.

Usually, the hardest part about these incidents was making sure we didn't all die of boredom before the all clear was sounded.

Kara and I were just getting into a good game on our phones when suddenly, a loud bang rang out from outside the room and the whole house seemed to shake.

"What the fuck?" I muttered, and my mother fixed a glare on me.

"Language, Logan! There are children present."

Oh, yeah. I glanced over at them in apology. "Sorry."

My ears were still ringing from the earlier noise as I strained to listen for any sounds from outside the room, and that's when I heard it.

A sawing, buzzing sound just on the other side of the door.

Someone was trying to cut their way in.

Chapter Seven

~~Logan's PoV~~

One year ago

"Evacuate!" I quickly ordered.

This was our backup plan and we had done it in drills, but never for real before. My heart was racing with actual fear now. How did the people on the other side of the door know we were in there? What did they want? We didn't have anything valuable, just women and children and a couple of older men with injuries that prevented them from fighting.

And me.

I ran to the rear of the room and opened the hidden door that led to the escape tunnel. Kara and my mom did their best to keep everyone calm as I helped them into the tunnel. We could see the edge of whatever tool the people at the door were using to cut through the door, but I did my best to keep my attention on the people instead.

"Logan." The fear in Kara's voice made me look up. The hole in the door was almost complete. In a matter of seconds they would push their way in and if the tunnel door was still open, they would see it and know where everyone had gone.

If I closed the door now, those that were already through would be safe but there were still a few people who weren't in yet.

I had to make a split-second decision, and as I helped the pack's cook into the tunnel, I made my choice.

I closed the door behind her, leaving three people still trapped in the room.

My mom, Kara and me.

My mom shifted into her wolf and I grabbed the only weapon I had access to, the hunting knife that my dad gave me that we'd mounted on the wall in here just in case. Holding it out in front of me, I shoved Kara behind me.

The men pushed through the hole in the door just a few seconds later. There were at least ten of them, half in their human form and the others as wolves.

We never had a chance.

My mom attacked while I stayed where I was, trying to protect Kara, but there were just too many of them. In less than a minute they had us all surrounded. One of them yanked the knife from my hand and held it up to my sister's throat as I struggled uselessly against the two men who were holding me.

"Shift," the man commanded my mother. "Or she dies."

With no other choice, my mom shifted back. Her leg was cut and bleeding and there were scratches across her face too.

"What do you want?" she asked the man, her voice shaking with rage or fear. Maybe both.

"I want to know who else was there the night it happened," the man said. "The night she appeared to you."

What the fuck did that mean? I had no clue but my mom's eyes went wide. "N-no one else was there," she stuttered, and even I could tell she was lying. "It was just me. Please, I'll tell you whatever you want to know about that night, just let my children go."

"This is your daughter?" The man looked down at Kara and my mom's face went completely white.

"No," she tried to lie, but it was too late. She'd already given it away.

"Kill them both."

Rage and shock raced through me and I let out a roar that made everyone stop and look at me in surprise. I didn't know where the strength came from but I was able to slip free of the men who were holding me and I went for the one with the knife. I got it from his hands and slit his throat before he could even raise a hand in self-defense.

But there were too many of them. As I turned around to face the others, someone hit me over the head with something hard, and the whole world went black.

When I woke up, it was to the sound of my father's cries of anguish. He was at the door, fallen to his knees, and my mother and sister were both dead.

~~Present~~

"I could have got them into the tunnel," I answered my father flatly as we stood in the garden. "It was my decision and they died because of me."

He put a hand on my shoulder and looked me straight in the face. "Logan, they died because those men killed them. They came here looking for your mother and your sister. They wouldn't have stopped until they found them."

"Why?"

That was the one question that had haunted me the most since that day. Why did they target my mom and Kara? What had they ever done to anyone to deserve that?

Why didn't they kill me too?

My dad just shook his head. "I don't know, but I will find out one day. And when I do, you and I will take them all down together."

The men who attacked us that day had gotten away. I was the only one who had seen their faces and lived to tell anyone about it.

"You saved the lives of everyone else in that room," he went on. "You did exactly what you were supposed to do. I know your mother and sister would be proud of you."

I hadn't let myself cry over this in so long, but as he said those words, I couldn't hold it in anymore. The tears came fast and hard, and my dad pulled me into a tight hug, letting me get it all out.

When I finally pulled away from him, I could see his face was wet too. My big, brave Alpha father. The only other time I had seen him cry was the day it happened.

"Micah's going to protect Sadie," he said firmly, reminding me of why we were out here in the first place. "But only because he's got his wolf. You're going to help me figure out who's after her, okay? And after you turn 18, if we still don't have answers, you can take over if you want to."

I nodded, not trusting myself to speak yet.

He started to walk away, but I called out after him with one last question. "Do you think this has anything to do with what happened to Mom and Kara?"

I didn't even know where the question came from, but as I thought about it now, I could see there were similarities. The sudden attack, the targeting of one person that they seemed to know exactly where to find.

My dad's face was tight. "I don't know, but you're going to help me find out."

And as I open the school doors this morning to step inside, that's exactly what I intend to do.

~~Sadie's PoV~~

By the time lunch comes, I'm ready for a break. Micah's been breathing down my neck all morning and I'm already tired of it.

Ava gives him a glare as he follows me into the cafeteria. "I don't think you need to be literally two steps behind her," she says to him.

"Don't tell me how to do my job," he snaps back before turning to me. "Do you need help getting lunch?"

What am I, five? "I think I can handle it," I answer sarcastically. "But I'll yell if I need you."

He nods like I was being serious, but thankfully, he goes to sit down next to Logan at the table and I breathe a sigh of relief.

"Are you surviving?" Ava asks as we join the line for food.

"It's actually kind of helpful," I say and she looks at me in surprise. "If I'm annoyed with him, I can't be too freaked out about being surrounded by werewolves."

She laughs at that. "I don't think you can complain about that when you're one of us too."

I keep forgetting that. It still doesn't feel real to me.

We get our lunch and go and join everyone else at the table. Aaron and Laurel are feeding each other grapes which is almost sickeningly sweet. Logan and Micah are talking to each other quietly while everyone else is making plans for the weekend.

It feels like any other day with any other kids in any other school. I have to keep reminding myself that it's not.

"How are you doing today, Sadie?" Logan asks, and everyone at the table immediately goes quiet, waiting for my answer.

My cheeks blush a little under all the attention. Or maybe it's just from the intense way Logan's looking at me. "I'm okay, thanks. And thank you for talking to me yesterday. I guess I was a bit too stunned to say it then."

I do appreciate that he told me the truth, even if it was a shock. He seems to respect me enough that he didn't want to lie to me.

He nods at me. "Let me give you my number in case you need to talk more."

There are rather excited murmurs and whispers among the rest of the group as I hand Logan my phone, which only makes me blush more. Why are they being so weird about this? He's just being friendly.

As if to prove my point, after he puts his number in my phone, he goes back to talking to Micah like the whole thing never happened. I chat with Ava and Blair and Tonya about Ava and Aaron's party and what everyone's going to wear. I feel like Blair's kind of giving me dirty looks, but she's probably just mad that Micah's going to be spending time with me. Ava told me they were dating. I want to tell her that it's not my choice, but I decide it's better not to mention it unless she says something to me directly.

After school, Micah insists on walking me home. "You're not going to watch over me as I sleep?" I ask him sarcastically. He's really taking this a little too far.

He shakes his head. "There's someone else assigned to watch your house at night."

There is? Suddenly, I feel a bit nervous. Having someone watch out for me at school, I kind of understand, but why do I need to be watched at night too? Couldn't my aunt and uncle watch out for me? I already know they can turn into wolves, I even saw my aunt do it.

I feel like there's something they're not telling me again, and it frustrates me.

"What makes me so special?" I wonder out loud. I don't know if Micah will even answer that, but he does, his face twisting a little into a sneer.

"You're not special, Sadie. You're weak. That's why you need to be protected. Being half-human makes you a liability to the pack."

"Well, fuck you too," I mutter under my breath. I don't really expect him to hear me, but he does and his face turns red.

"You can't talk to me like that," he says, grabbing my arm so I stop walking. He looks down at me with a serious, angry look. "I'm the future Beta of the pack. Maybe you don't know what that means, so I'll tell you. It's the second most important position after the Alpha. Well, and the Luna, I guess, if we still had one. But it means everyone else in the pack has to respect me and do as I say, and that includes you."

"Well, you're not Beta yet, are you?" I shoot back. "So I don't have to do anything. And maybe because I'm half-human, I don't actually have to do what you guys say at all. Did you ever consider that?"

His nostrils flare in anger, but he lets me go. "You still don't understand," he mutters, his eyes dark as he looks down at me.

"That you're an asshole? Actually, I figured that out on day one. It was the only thing here that wasn't a mystery to me."

"Sadie!" Ava's voice calls out from behind us before Micah can answer and I see his jaw clenching in frustration. "I was looking for you, but you left so fast. You want to go dress shopping for my party?"

I glance over at Micah and he understands my unspoken question. "If you do, then I'm coming too."

I roll my eyes. "No, thanks," I tell Ava. "I've got stuff I can wear. Let's just go home."

We finally get to the front door. Micah goes over to talk to a man standing on the sidewalk, and I guess he's the one that will be watching the house while I'm at home. This is all so weird. I look back one last time before I close the door behind me and Micah's still watching me. I shut the door.

The rest of the week goes pretty quickly. I almost get into a routine. Micah gets on my nerves a few times, but we don't get into any full-on arguments. There's actually even one or two times that he laughs at something I say, though he quickly tries to pretend like he didn't. I have to admit he can even be a little funny too when he's talking to his friends and not just being a jerk to me.

Finally, it's Saturday morning, the day of Ava and Aaron's party, and I'm woken up by a frantic knock on my door.

"Sadie?" Ava's voice calls through the door. "Emergency! I need your help!"

~~**Ava's PoV**~~

Sadie opens the door, her eyes wide and her hair sticking out at crazy angles. She obviously just got out of bed. "Emergency?" she repeats. "Is there another wolf attack?"

Oh, shit. I didn't mean to scare her. "No, no, no, nothing like that! Sorry. I just can't find the earrings I was going to wear tonight."

Sadie lets out a deep breath and glares at me. "Seriously, Ava? You had to wake me up for that?"

"I didn't know you were still in bed," I protest. "But now that you're up..."

I hook my arm through hers and pull her into my room. Her eyes go even wider as she looks around.

"You're surprised you can't find your earrings? How do you find anything in here? It's a disaster."

That's a bit of an exaggeration, I think, as I step over some piles of clothes. "I was trying them on the other night to make sure they went with my dress and now they're gone. Please, Sadie, I need your help!"

She sighs but gives in, digging into the things on top of my dresser.

It takes us nearly half an hour but finally we find them as well as all my other accessories for the evening. I ask Sadie again what she's going to wear but she just tells me I'll see it when she's ready. When I first heard Sadie was coming to live with us, I thought it was going to be fun having another girl in the house but Sadie seems to care less about clothes and makeup than Aaron does, and that's saying something.

Sadie goes back to her room to get dressed for the day and I head downstairs where my mom is making a special brunch to celebrate our birthday.

"Happy birthday, baby girl!" she greets me with a big smile and a hug. "Are you ready for today?"

"So ready!" I've been waiting for this day for so long. By the end of the day, I'll meet my wolf and, hopefully, my mate too! Who wouldn't be ready for that?

Aaron comes down soon too and Mom gives him the same hug, calling him her baby boy even though he towers over her now. He rolls his eyes at me but I can see he's excited too.

When Sadie and my dad join us too, we all sit down for waffles and bacon and eggs. "Exactly how many people are coming to this party?" Sadie asks.

It's one of the first things she's asked me about today, so I answer giddily. "Just about the whole pack! Even the Alpha is coming, you'll finally get to meet him!"

I can see she's curious about that. "Does he go to everyone's birthday parties?"

We all laugh at that and Sadie looks confused, so I try to explain it to her. "No, there's way too many for him to go to all of them, but Dad is the pack's head warrior. He works closely with the Alpha, they're good friends, even though we're not one of the ranked families."

"Ranked?" Sadie repeats. "What does that mean?"

This is one of the things I've been willing to tell her about but she hasn't asked me until now. I'm glad she's finally taking an interest.

"Well, I already told you about how the Alpha is a hereditary position, right? So are the other highest ranks, the Beta and the Gamma. Those positions usually stay within the same families unless something happens, so those families are ranked as most important in the pack. Then there are other positions like the Epsilons and the warrior roles like Dad's that are earned by merit."

Sadie wrinkles her nose. "It all sounds really old-fashioned. Why should someone get to be in charge just because they were born to particular parents?"

"It's in their blood," my dad steps in to explain. "Humans have evolved in a different way where the blood isn't so important, but for wolves, our blood gives us different abilities. An Alpha's bloodline will be stronger and bigger and more powerful than other wolves so they are naturally more gifted to lead. It gives the pack greater stability than if there were constantly people fighting over the position."

Sadie looks conflicted. "I guess that makes sense, I just think it's kind of sad that you don't get any choice. You have to be whatever position you're born to, you have to marry whoever your wolf says, it's like you don't get to make any decisions for yourself at all!"

Her voice raises at the end and the rest of us all exchange glances. Maybe she's not taking the werewolf news quite as well as we all thought she was.

"Maybe you could talk to Logan about it," I suggest, remembering how he gave Sadie his number the other day. I don't think she's reached out to him yet, but he would be a good person to explain how the whole rank system works. "As the Alpha's son, he knows more about it than anyone."

Sadie looks at me with wide eyes. "Logan is the Alpha's son?"

Didn't I ever tell her that? I try to think back but I can't remember for sure. I guess not, then. "Yeah, so he's going to be the next Alpha. He can tell you all about it."

"I think that's a great idea," my mom chimes in. "Ava and Aaron, you can go with your dad to set up everything for the party, and Sadie, you can invite Logan over here if you want to."

We agree and as soon as brunch is over, we all split up. I give Sadie a hug and tell her I'll be back later so we can get ready together. Hopefully by the time I see her again, she'll be feeling a lot better about the whole thing.

Chapter Eight

~~Sadie's PoV~~

My heart beats a little faster as I dial Logan's number, even though I try to tell myself it's no big deal. He said I could call him if I needed to talk, and that's all I'm doing. It's nothing more than that, even if my body doesn't seem to agree.

He answers on the third ring. "Hey, Sadie," his deep voice says through the phone. "What's up?"

For some reason, my mouth has gone dry, but I try to answer normally. "Hi, Logan. I'm sorry to bug you, but I had some questions about the whole pack life thing, and Ava reminded me that you said I could talk to you. If you're busy, it's okay, you don't have to…"

He cuts me off before I can finish. "I'm not busy. Give me a few minutes and I'll come over."

He hangs up before I can say anything else and I stare at my phone in surprise for a second. I didn't really expect him to be so eager about it but it makes me feel a bit better. I go back to my room just to double check my hair and makeup and the girl in the mirror looks back at me in amusement. What do I think is going to happen when he comes over? He's already the best-looking guy I've ever met in real life, and now I just found out he's pretty much a prince, or whatever the hell they call the heir to the Alpha. He's never going to think of me as anything more than a friend, and that's if I'm lucky.

So why have the butterflies in my stomach gone into overdrive at the idea of being alone with him?

I try to keep busy so I don't get too nervous until there's a knock at the door. I hear my aunt's voice from downstairs. "Hi, Logan, thank you for coming over."

"It's my pleasure, Mrs Miller," I hear him reply respectfully. "I can imagine this has all been challenging for Sadie. I'm happy to help if I can."

I'm torn between a bit of annoyance that he thinks I need help and gratitude that he wants to help me. I can't decide which feeling is stronger.

"Sadie?" my aunt calls up the stairs. "Logan's here."

Ava already told me her mom doesn't let boys go upstairs (or girls, in Aaron's case), so I head down. My own parents were never that strict, they trusted me to make my own choices. I had a couple of boyfriends at my old school and we fooled around a few times in my room, but I haven't gone all the way with anyone yet. And now, it seems like my first time might end up being with a werewolf? What's that like, I wonder? Are they rougher in bed, more like animals?

I catch sight of Logan just as I start to blush from the thoughts in my head, and the sight of him makes me blush harder. He looks really good, dressed in a black t-shirt that shows off the defined muscles of his arms and stretches across the hard plane of his chest. His sandy hair is a bit wet, like he just washed it, and he smells fresh like the cedar trees that used to grow in the park by my old house.

It takes me a second to realize I'm staring. "Hi," I try to say casually. "Thanks for making time for me."

He just nods. "Should we go sit down somewhere?"

I lead him into the living room and we sit down on opposite ends of the couch. I can hear my aunt moving around in the kitchen, getting things ready for the party, but I trust that she'll leave us alone to talk.

"So, what can I help with?" he asks me as he settles back into the couch. his green eyes watching me curiously.

I explain to him what Ava told me this morning about the ranked families and how everyone's position is already defined for them. "It just all seems a bit weird to me," I admit. "What if you don't want to be Alpha?"

He almost smiles, just one side of his mouth turning up. "Of course I want to be Alpha. It's a big privilege to be able to lead the pack and protect them."

"But maybe you only feel that way because you've been told your whole life that you have to," I pointed out. "It's like some kind of conditioning to take away your free will."

His smile gets a little bigger. "Nobody's being conditioned, Sadie. You make it sound like we're some kind of cult."

"It kind of feels that way," I admit, and he laughs. He actually laughs. It's the first time I've heard his laugh and it gives me a strange, tingling feeling throughout my whole body.

He looks almost as surprised as I am that the sound came out of him, but he gives his head a little shake and answers me. "I get why it feels a bit weird to you, I honestly do, but it's not like that. There's comfort and security in knowing your place in the world, knowing where your skills are most useful."

I'm still not convinced. "But you only think that because you always knew that you would be Alpha."

The smile leaves his face entirely. "Actually, that's not true. I was never supposed to be Alpha."

He wasn't? A vague memory crosses my mind, something Ava said about how the next Alpha was supposed to be a girl? I can't remember exactly.

"Who was?" I blurt out before I think it through, and I immediately regret it when I see a flash of pain cross his face. I apologize right away. "I'm sorry. If it's not any of my business, you don't have to tell me."

Logan takes a breath. "No, it's okay, you'll hear about it eventually. My sister Kara was supposed to be Alpha, she was the one who grew up thinking she would be. I always thought I would work with her to support her, but she'd be the one in charge."

"What happened?" I ask quietly. I don't know for sure how it works, but if it's like other hereditary positions, the only way she wouldn't be Alpha anymore would be if she was no longer alive. Was that what that look of pain meant?

Logan quickly confirms my fears. "She died a year ago. We were attacked and she and my mother were killed."

"Fuck," I swear before I can stop myself, and just for a second, there's a look of recognition on Logan's face, an unspoken understanding.

"Yeah," he agrees with a small shrug. "That's all you can say, right?"

I know he's talking about my parents too, so I nod in agreement. There aren't any words that make it better, no matter how hard people try, so I don't even try. Instead I just reach out and put my hand on top of his.

He looks down at it in surprise, but he doesn't move away. For a moment, we just sit there, our hands touching. His hand feels warm and solid beneath my fingers and there's a little tingle there too, almost like static electricity.

Finally, he looks back up at me again. "Have you ever shot a gun?"

I pull my hand back and blink in surprise. Where the hell did that come from? "No," I answer honestly. "Why?"

He nods, like he's decided on something. "It helps me sometimes, just to get the frustration out. Come on, let's go to the pack house. We've got a range there. I'll teach you."

~~**Aaron's PoV**~~

Ava and I get back from setting up the party and I go upstairs to get ready. I've been having this weird feeling for the last hour or so, like there's someone standing just behind me, just out of sight. It must mean my wolf is getting ready to come out. I really can't wait.

I get dressed in a dark blue shirt and black dress pants. The blue is Laurel's favorite color on me, she always says it brings out my eyes so I want to be wearing it when she sees I'm her mate. I can't wait for that either.

When I'm ready, I go back downstairs where Mom and Dad are already waiting but it takes a lot longer for Sadie and Ava to show up. When they do, Ava's dressed up like she's going to some red-carpet Hollywood party. She's wearing a slinky red dress with high heeled shoes that I'm sure have a specific name but I have no idea what it is. Her blonde hair is pulled up with ringlets hanging down and she's got sparkly diamond earrings and a matching necklace.

"Looking good, sis," I tell her genuinely. I know she's just as excited about tonight as I am.

She looks me over and brushes something off my shoulder, though I'm sure there was nothing there. "What did you spend getting ready, five minutes?"

"Yup," I agree, giving her a cheeky smile, and she glares at me. Sometimes, it's really good to be a man. I turn to Sadie, not wanting to leave her out. "You look great too, Sadie."

She's far less formal than Ava, wearing an off the shoulder dress that's black on top with a black and pink skirt. Once again, I'm no fashion expert, but I think she looks nice. Her dark hair is mostly down, with a few braids through it, and she's got more makeup on than usual. She's also smiling more than she has been in the last couple of weeks, so that's nice to see.

My mom insists on pictures out in front of the house so we all go and pose until she's satisfied and finally, we head over to the lake for the party.

It's the first time Sadie's been to the lake and she looks around curiously as we pull up. "This is all still part of the pack territory?"

I'm a bit surprised by the question, I didn't think she knew much about the territory, but I guess she and Logan must have had a good talk earlier. "Yeah," I answer her. "We've got a big territory, we're one of the biggest packs around. This is a good pack to be part of, you'll see."

"Aaron!" I turn to see Laurel arriving with her parents and my heart nearly skips a beat at the sight of her. She's the most beautiful girl I've ever seen and when she's dressed up like she is tonight, she literally takes my breath away.

I listen carefully inside my head for a second, hoping my wolf will choose this moment to tell me that she's my mate, but there's nothing there. Usually, wolves don't appear until sundown, when the moon comes up, but I was hoping maybe mine would be a bit early.

"You look amazing," I tell her honestly, giving her a small kiss. I'd love to kiss her more, but we have a pretty big audience. I say hi to her parents and we all go to the tables that we set up earlier.

More people start to arrive and before long just about the whole pack is here. I lose track of where everyone is as we all mingle with everyone and eat the amazing food my mom made. The only one I keep my eye on is Laurel, who never leaves my side. Whenever I catch sight of Ava, she seems to be having fun too, and so does Sadie, except for one time when I see her arguing with Micah. I'm about to go over and see what's going on when the Alpha suddenly appears in front of me.

"Happy birthday, Aaron," he says to me, and I bow my head in appreciation.

"Thank you, Alpha." It's a real honor that he's here at our party.

"We'll be seeing you out on the training field in the morning, I hope?" he asks seriously, and I almost panic.

I don't have to start training tomorrow, do I? I thought because of the party tonight that I was getting the day off and I would start on Monday instead.

He laughs at the look on my face. "I'm just kidding, you've got the day off tomorrow. But we're all excited to have you and your wolf join the team."

I breathe a sigh of relief. "I'm looking forward to it too. Thank you, sir."

My mom calls out for everyone to gather around and we all move over to where she's standing. "It's almost sunset," she announces proudly. "Ava and Aaron, come over and meet your wolves."

Ava and I both make our way through the crowd. I've seen this happen dozens of times before at other people's parties, but now that it's my turn, I'm a bit nervous. We get to the front and I take Ava's hand, partly to give her support and partly to help steady myself too.

The sun disappears over the horizon and my skin starts to tingle. There's a warm feeling all through my body and suddenly, a voice speaks inside my head. *Aaron.*

I know it's my wolf, at last, and I answer him internally. *What's your name?*

Blaze, he replies, and I smile. That's a good, strong name. I like it.

I ask him the question I want answered more than anything in the world. *Do you see our mate?*

Together, we look out over the crowd and as our eyes fall on Laurel, I wait for the confirmation from him, but there's only silence.

"Mate?" Laurel says, her voice full of confusion.

I'm confused too, my heart racing with panic. Why don't I feel it? What's going on?

And then I realize she's not looking at me at all.

She's looking right at Ava.

~~Logan's PoV~~

There's a moment of shocked silence at the party when Laurel calls out to Ava as her mate.

Aaron looks devastated, Ava and Laurel are confused, and my eyes immediately meet my dad's and he nods at me, agreeing with my unspoken conclusion.

Whatever is going on at the other packs must be affecting us too.

"Everyone, please excuse us for a minute," my dad announces, his strong Alpha voice carrying across all the gathered guests. "We'll be back shortly for Ava and Aaron's first shift."

He gathers Ava, Aaron, their parents, and Laurel and her parents, and leads them all away from the party. I follow after them and so does Beta Aldric, Micah, and Sadie. I don't know if Sadie should necessarily be a part of this, but as soon as the Beta turns and orders her to go, I can't stop myself from standing up for her.

"They're her cousins," I point out to him. "And it's fine with me if she stays."

His lips tighten in disagreement but he doesn't directly contradict me. He turns his attention back to my dad instead as the Alpha starts to speak to the whole group.

"I believe this mating bond might be in error," he tells everyone. "Unless, Ava and Laurel disagree?"

The girls look at each other awkwardly. "I'm pretty sure I'm straight," Ava says almost apologetically. "And even if I wasn't, Laurel's been dating Aaron so long, she's like my own sister. I'm definitely not attracted to her. Sorry, Laurel."

Laurel almost laughs in relief. "Trust me, I feel the same way, Ava." She turns back to my dad. "But Alpha, how can it be wrong? I don't understand. My wolf is telling me that Ava's my mate. She's sure of it."

My dad sighs. "I don't know, but it's not the first time it's happened lately, though it's the first time here in our pack. I didn't want anyone to panic so I haven't shared it with the pack yet, but maybe we'll need to. We might need to put all mating on hold until we figure out what's behind it."

"How long will that be?" Aaron asks, and I can hear the desperation in his voice. I really feel bad for him, he was so certain that Laurel is his mate and now he'll have to wait even longer to find out for sure. If we are ever even able to figure it out, I can't help adding in my head. What happens if we can't?

"I don't know, Aaron," my dad says sympathetically. "I wish I had the answers, but I don't. For now, let's go back to the party and you can do your shift. In the morning, I'll make an announcement to the pack about the temporary hold on mating."

His words are an order rather than a suggestion so everyone bows their heads and most of them head back to the party. My dad and Aldric move away to speak to each other, and Micah and Sadie both stay with me, both of them looking at me as if I might know more than what they just heard.

"So, let me get this straight," Sadie says slowly. "Not only do you have to marry whoever your wolf tells you to, but they might not even be right?"

I know she's got issues with a lot of pack life, we talked about it a bit today, and I admit this really doesn't help my case.

After we talked at her aunt and uncle's house, I took her to the shooting range at the pack house like I'd promised. We walked over there together. The weather had started to turn warmer, there was hardly any snow left and soon, flowers would be starting to grow. I hadn't thought about flowers in a while. It seemed I was remembering a lot of things I hadn't thought about for a while recently.

At the range, I handed Sadie a small handgun. "This is the safety," I pointed out to her. "Keep that on at all times until you're ready to shoot."

"Like this?" she asked, holding the gun out with one hand like they do in the movies.

"Only if you want to knock yourself over with the kickback," I replied drily. "So, no. Use both hands, like this."

I placed my hands on top of hers to guide them into the proper position, and just like it had at her house, my skin tingled a little at the contact.

What did that mean? It took me completely by surprise when it first happened. Neither of us had our wolves yet, we shouldn't be feeling mating sparks yet even if she was my mate, which there was no way of knowing yet. Did it have something to do with the strange things that were happening with mates in the surrounding packs? I had no idea, so I decided it was safer to ignore it for now. She didn't say anything about it either, so maybe she didn't even feel it. Maybe it was all in my head.

When I got her positioned correctly, I showed her how to remove the safety and aim. "When you're ready, just pull the trigger towards you."

She began to, her eyes closing in anticipation of the discharge, and I quickly called out again.

"Wait. Keep your eyes open, keep aiming until it fires. Look at that target down there like it's the thing you hate most in the world, the thing that makes you the angriest. Then stare it down as you take the shot."

Sadie looked over at me curiously, the gun still aiming towards the target. "What do you imagine it is?"

That was an easy one. "The wolves that attacked us last year."

I saw them in front of me every time I pulled the trigger. The face of the one in charge was seared into my memory like a brand. If I ever saw him again, one of us was ending up dead, and I was pretty sure it wasn't going to be me.

Sadie nodded and looked back at the target. "Nobody killed my parents," she said quietly. "There's nobody to blame. It was just a stupid accident."

"Then pretend that target is the road," I suggested. "Or the car they were driving. Whatever caused the accident to happen."

She nodded again and straightened her stance. Her face set in concentration as she stared the target down and pulled the trigger.

I can almost hear the gunshot again as I look over at her now, next to the lake along with Micah.

"Nobody's getting forced to be with anyone they don't want to be with," I point out. "We'll figure out what's happening and we'll fix it."

I sound a lot more confident about that than I am. The truth is I'm nervous, not only for Aaron and Ava and Laurel and the rest of the pack, but for myself too. After all, my 18th birthday is coming up too. What if my mate is right in front of me and I never know it?

Chapter Nine

~~Micah's PoV~~

I know everyone is a little freaked out by the mating surprise, but I can't help being a little excited. This is a real-life mystery for me to get involved in. As the future Beta, pack security is my main responsibility, and I always thought that if I were a human, I would have been a detective, solving crimes and figuring out puzzles. This looks like the perfect opportunity to use all my skills and show everyone just how much I bring to this pack.

Especially my dad. He'll have to be impressed with me if I figure this out before anyone else does.

Sadie stands next to me with her arms crossed while Logan assures her we'll get to the bottom of what's happening. She hasn't even glanced over at me this whole time. I know she's a little bit annoyed with me because of our argument earlier, but the truth is I'm annoyed too.

She had been standing and talking to Emma and Alison from school and I was nearby, keeping an eye on her, as I was supposed to be doing. They were talking about men even though they knew I could hear them. It felt like they were doing it on purpose to see if they could get me to leave, but I wouldn't abandon my post that easily. They started listing off all the hottest guys in our class and didn't mention me. I knew it was on purpose because Emma kept glancing over at me to see how I was going to react, but I didn't give them the satisfaction.

But then Alison said something that made me intervene.

"Logan's been looking over at you all night," she said to Sadie. "Maybe he'll be your mate!"

The words felt like something sharp scraping against my insides, and I couldn't stop myself from interrupting. "Sadie can't be Logan's mate. The next Alpha would never be mated to someone who's only half a wolf."

Sadie's eyes went darker than normal as she looked over at me angrily and a rush of longing went through me. Why did that look turn me on? The way my body behaved around her really didn't make any sense to me.

We argued about whether humans or wolves were better, but it wasn't the argument that upset me.

It was the idea of Logan and Sadie being mates.

If I was being honest, I didn't care if Logan was mated to a human or a hybrid or a fucking leprechaun for that matter. I just didn't want him mated to Sadie.

Everything about her confused and disoriented me, but I felt protective of her too. I didn't understand it at all.

We all walk back to the party, and soon Ava and Aaron go back to the front to do their first shift. I just did this myself a few months ago so I remember exactly what it felt like. The person, or in this case people, about to shift puts on special tear-away clothes that are designed for this occasion. Then, they have to talk to their wolf and convince them to come out. Sometimes, it's easy. My wolf was so excited to come out, I hardly had to say anything to him at all. Other people's wolves take more coaxing.

Tonight, Aaron shifts pretty quickly. I can't help watching Sadie's reactions as his body begins to transform, his bones snapping and his claws growing and the fur sprouting from his skin. She covers her mouth like she's watching a horror movie instead of the most exciting moment in a werewolf's life.

Ava takes longer. Her frown grows deeper the longer she waits, letting me know that she must be arguing with her wolf. Finally, she looks over at her mother, almost in tears. "My wolf doesn't want to come out until I claim my mate," she whispers, but from where I'm standing, I can hear it too.

I step over towards her, surprising us both.

"What do you want?" she asks defensively. Normally, Ava and I get along okay but I know she's pissed with me lately about Sadie, so I put up my hands in a gesture of peace.

"Just close your eyes, Ava," I instruct her. "Smell the trees and the earth. Help your wolf think about what it'll be like to run and feel the world in that form."

She still looks a little suspicious of me, but she does what I say. Her breathing starts to relax.

"The moon is out," I continue, talking directly to her wolf. "It'll shine down on your fur and give you strength. You'll be strong and healthy and your mate will be so impressed."

That seems to be what she needed to hear. Ava cries out in pain as the shift begins and I step back to where I was. I glance over at Sadie and she's giving me a look of surprise and maybe even a little respect.

I like her looking at me that way. Better than when she's annoyed with me, anyway.

Once the shift and their first runs are done, Ava and Aaron shift back and the party starts to break up.

The Alpha comes over to me before he leaves. "That was good work with Ava," he tells me, nodding with approval. "Come to my office tomorrow with your dad, we'll be coming up with a plan to investigate the mate bond problem."

Pride surges through me, both at the praise and at being included in the meeting tomorrow. "Yes, sir," I answer firmly.

Once he leaves, I look around with satisfaction. Despite what happened with Ava and Laurel, and even in spite of my little fight with Sadie, this actually ended up being a really good party.

~~Sadie's PoV~~

I'm exhausted by the time we get home after the party and as soon as I change out of my dress into my pajamas, I fall straight into bed. However, it isn't long before I'm woken by a whimpering, whining sound outside my door.

Still half asleep, I get up to open it only to find a grey and white wolf there. That wakes me up fast enough and I take a couple of panicked steps back before it starts whimpering again, and I realize that whoever it is, they're not here to hurt me. They're just upset.

I take a deep breath to try to slow my racing heart and look at the wolf closer. I've seen this wolf before.

"Ava?"

It was like she was waiting for me to invite her in. The wolf comes into my room and jumps up on my bed, taking up half the bed as she puts her head down and looks up at me with sad eyes.

What am I supposed to do now? It's like she's come to talk, but I don't speak wolf. Do they even have a language? How do they talk to each other? There are still so many things I don't know.

"Are you okay?" I ask as I take a step closer to her. She doesn't look so dangerous close up. She looks a lot like a big dog, especially with those pleading eyes.

She just whimpers again and looks down, and I try to think back to the few things I know about werewolves so far and what happened tonight.

It must be something to do with her mate.

I still don't really get how Ava's wolf can be wrong about who her mate is, but at least I'm not the only one who seems confused by it. My aunt tells me it's never happened before. Even Logan's dad seemed unsure.

The Alpha is a big, tough-looking guy, but when Logan and I ran into him at their house after we'd finished our shooting lesson, he was actually really nice to me. He greeted me kindly when Logan introduced me and said he remembers my mom well. He told me that she and Logan's mom were good friends growing up. Logan looked surprised at that and I didn't know about it either, but then I really don't know anything about my mom's childhood. I guess she never told me much so that she wouldn't have to explain about werewolves. Or maybe I just never asked. It's hard to know.

Anyway, the Alpha seemed as surprised as anyone earlier tonight when Ava and Laurel thought they were mates, so I don't know how I can help when even the people who are supposed to know all about this stuff don't know what to do. But I try my best anyway, sitting down on the bed next to Ava's wolf and scratching her ears like she's actually a dog.

It seems to help a little bit. Her whimpering stops, at least, as her head leans into my hand.

"Look, Ava, I don't know how all this stuff works," I tell her, feeling more than a little weird about talking to the giant dog on my bed like it's my cousin, but at this point I'm just going to go for it. "But I don't see why you have to be with anyone just because some goddess chose them for you. You're a strong, smart, beautiful woman... at least when you're not a wolf... and you can be with whoever you want to be with."

The wolf starts to move beneath my hand and I quickly pull it away as I realize it's turning back into my cousin. The fur disappears into her skin, her claws turn back into fingernails, and Ava's face emerges from the wolf's face, but her sad eyes are still the same.

I grab an extra blanket from my closet for her to wrap around herself and sit down on the bed again.

"Thanks, Sadie," she says. "But you don't understand. I *want* my mate. I want to find the person I'm supposed to be with. My wolf is sad because I don't believe her, and I'm sad because she's wrong. It's awful to be fighting with a part of yourself."

She's right about one thing: I really don't understand. "So you actually talk to your wolf? Like, with words?"

Ava nods. "It's all in my head, but yeah. We have a regular conversation, just like this. And now she won't let me sleep because she wants to go and be with our mate, who isn't really our mate."

"Well, you heard the Alpha tonight," I remind her. "He says they'll figure it out. And Logan told me that too."

"I hope so." She looks so sad that I have to give her a hug, which is interrupted by another knock on my still-open door.

"Is this the room for people who are upset about tonight?"

Aaron stands at the doorway looking just as sad as Ava, maybe even more. We both scoot over to make room for him on the bed.

"I'm really sorry, Aaron," Ava says. "I didn't mean for this to happen."

"I know that, Ava. It's not your fault at all. Don't feel bad about me, okay? I just feel bad for Laurel."

Looking at both their sad faces, I make a decision. If I don't do something, they're just going to sit here and feel sorry for themselves all night. I've done enough of that in the last few weeks to know it's not always the best idea.

Going shooting with Logan today was actually really good for me. For the first time in a long time, I felt like I had some control over something in my life.

Obviously, we can't go shooting in the middle of the night, but there must be something we could do.

"Come on," I tell them both, jumping to my feet. "We're going outside."

"What?" Ava asks.

"Why?" Aaron says at almost the same time.

"Those wolves of yours need something to do besides drive you both crazy. So, let's go find something for them to do."

~~Ava's PoV~~

Sadie's suggestion takes me completely by surprise. It's the middle of the night and she wants to go outside? But when she explains it's to help my wolf, I feel Spark start to stir hopefully inside me. She wants to go out too.

I'm still getting used to the feeling of having a completely different being inside me, not to mention one that's completely pissed off at me. Spark had barely told me her name when she suddenly howled and told me that Laurel was our mate.

Shocked isn't a strong enough word to describe how I felt. As I told the Alpha afterwards, I've never been attracted to other girls. And even if I was, it definitely wouldn't be Laurel. After all the time she's spent kissing my brother? Gross.

So, when he told us it was all a mistake, I was very, very relieved, but I didn't know how to explain it to the heartbroken wolf inside me who was 100% sure that she was right and I was wrong.

I throw some clothes back on and the three of us sneak down the stairs quietly so we don't wake my parents. Sadie puts her hand on the doorknob to open it when Aaron suddenly whispers, "Wait!"

Sadie and I both freeze. "What?" I hiss back at him.

"There's a guard outside," he reminds us. "Watching over the house because of Sadie."

Oh, right. Our parents told us that, though they couldn't really say why. Just that it was Alpha's orders, which meant we had to agree.

"I'll distract him," I offer. "And you two can sneak out the back."

Aaron nods and he and Sadie go to the back of the house while I open the front door and march out like it's a totally normal thing to be doing.

"Ava?" The guard is a guy named Rory who's just a few years older than me. I remember him from when he was still in school with us. "What are you doing out here?"

"I just got my wolf," I tell him, sticking as close to the truth as possible. "And she wants to go for a walk."

"Oh, right. Happy birthday, by the way," he says, though it's technically not my birthday anymore.

"Thanks." I glance towards the back of the house where Sadie and Aaron are sneaking across the lawn. Rory starts to turn to follow my look, so I quickly speak again to make him look at me. "So, they make you just stand out here all night, huh?"

Rory isn't amused. "Nobody makes me do anything. It's my job and I'm happy to do it if it's what the pack needs."

"What are you even looking for?" I ask, genuinely curious. "What does Sadie need to be protected from?"

"That's restricted information," he answers, but I can see the little tug at his lips as he says it. He doesn't know either.

That should be enough time for Aaron and Sadie to get away. "Okay, well, I'm just going to go for a short run now. I'll be back soon."

"Stay safe, Ava," he advises. "If there's any kind of alert, come right home."

Now that I have my wolf, I'll be able to hear the pack-wide mind-link alerts now. I forgot about that. I promise Rory I'll do just that and I head off down the street where I find Sadie and Aaron waiting for me around the corner.

"Let's hope you don't actually need protecting," I grin at Sadie. "Because it was way too easy to get past that guard."

As I get closer, I realize she's got a bicycle with her. I think it's mine. She sees me looking at it and smiles. "I won't be able to run fast enough to keep up with you two, right? But this way I can try."

There's a trail just at the edge of town, not far from our house, so we head over there, the light of the moon showing us the way. My wolf feels happier under the moonlight. She's not whimpering quite so much.

CLAIMING MY WOLF

When we get to the edge of the trees, Aaron and I both strip down for the shift while Sadie looks away. I'm used to seeing naked people because of all the shifting that happens. It's weird sometimes when it's your own parents or something, but you get used to it after a while. Sadie will get used to it too, I'm sure.

Once we shift, Sadie hops on the bike and leads the way, using the bike's headlight and setting the pace through the forest. I already feel a lot better as Spark starts to run and I wonder if Aaron feels better too.

I'm still upset, his voice says in my head. *But yeah, it's a bit better.*

Whoa. I must have mind-linked my thoughts to him without even meaning to. This is going to take some getting used to.

We run for at least twenty minutes, up to the lake before we start to come back. I talk to Spark as we go, telling her about the pack and all the guys who might be our actual mate, trying to get her to let go of the idea of Laurel, but it's no use. She won't budge. At least she's not crying about it anymore though. The run takes too much energy.

We're about ten minutes from home when the alert comes.

Breach at the border. Everyone take your defensive positions.

Shit. Aaron and I look at each other, not sure what to do now. We've got defensive positions at home and at school, but out here in the woods, the instruction is just to conceal yourself as much as possible and cover your scent.

We need to get Sadie's attention. She's still pedaling on her bike, not aware of anything. I let out a howl to get her to stop, and Aaron quickly glares at me.

What was that for? You just gave away our position!

Oh, fuck, he's right, I didn't think about that. *I just needed Sadie to stop.*

At least she did. She hops off the bike and comes back to us where we stopped. "Is everything okay? Did you hurt yourself?"

I can't answer her like I am, obviously, so I shift back. "I'm okay but we just got an alert. We're going to need to hide."

"Hide?" Sadie said, her eyes widening as she looks around the moonlit forest. "Do you mean there are other wolves out here? Not friendly ones?"

I don't want to scare her, but I can't lie either. "Maybe. But come on, you've got two wolves to protect you now. It's going to be fine."

I don't mention that Aaron and I have never had any kind of training in our wolf forms. This is all brand new to us.

We leave the bike by the path and move further into the trees until we find a good hiding place. I find some strong-smelling plants, like my mother taught me, and place them all around our position, hoping that will overpower our own scents.

Then, I shift back to my wolf and Aaron and I sit on either side of Sadie, keeping our eyes and ears open. There's nothing we can do now but wait.

Chapter Ten

~~Logan's PoV~~

I should be asleep but my mind is refusing to rest. I keep thinking over everything that happened in the last week. The mate mess is top priority for me as the future Alpha, but there's also the attack on the school, targeting Sadie. And then there's Sadie herself and the way she's managed to bring me out of myself like no one else succeeded in doing over the last year.

I'm still confused by the tingling feelings I had when we touched earlier, but the other feelings I have are getting clearer all the time.

I like her. I like the way she doesn't hesitate to say what she's thinking. I like that I feel comfortable telling her things, and I like when she opens up to me too. And she's pretty too, in a totally natural and unassuming way. There was a moment at the gun range earlier when I watched her grin as she took another shot at the target, and I actually wondered what it would be like to kiss her.

These are all things I haven't felt for any girl in a long time. My whole life is divided into before the attack and after. In the 'before' time, I used to go on dates. I never got serious with anyone, but I dated. I kissed some girls. I didn't do a lot more because I was still young and because I didn't want to lead anyone on. As the Alpha's son, I can't just go around sleeping with anyone I feel like and getting anyone's hopes up. That's not how my mother raised me, and my sister would have kicked my ass if I broke anyone's heart.

So, it was all pretty innocent before. And after... well, I haven't even thought about dating anyone. What right did I have to do things like dating and kissing and enjoying my life when Kara would never get to see another day?

That hasn't changed, and yet somehow, it has. Kara would like Sadie, I'm sure of it. I can almost hear my sister in my head, telling me not to be an idiot and not to waste my own life mourning hers.

But am I really ready to do that? It feels like such a big step, though maybe not quite as big as it felt just a week ago.

I roll over to try to get comfortable and that's when the alarm goes off in the pack house. Immediately, I jump out of bed and run down to my dad's office, wearing only my pajama pants.

I'm no longer in charge of securing the house. My dad took that job away from me at my own request. Technically, I should be the one being secured, just as my sister was before, but when I rush into his office, my dad doesn't send me away.

"What's going on?" I ask, looking between him and the other men already gathered. Gamma Ellis is here, mind-linking with the defense team. Beta Aldric isn't here yet because he doesn't live in the house, but I'm sure he's on the way.

"More intruders," my dad grimaces to me before going back to barking orders at the others.

"Sadie?" I ask, taking another step towards him.

My dad turns back to me. "The guard on duty hasn't seen anything. She's fine for now and we've sent reinforcements."

"Actually, Alpha," Gamma Ellis interrupts nervously. "I've just heard from Anderson Miller. He went to check on his family when he got the alert and they're all gone. The twins and Sadie."

"Fuck," my dad swears under his breath before his own eyes glaze over. It isn't long before he slams his palm down on the desk in frustration. "I can't link to the twins, they're probably too overwhelmed to know how to control it yet. Ellis, send the tracking team to the Miller house. They should be able to follow their scents."

I head towards the door too but he calls out to stop me.

"Logan, you can't leave the house. It's not safe."

I know he's right, but I also know that I'm going. I just need a wolf to come along. "I'll take Micah with me."

As if I summoned him, he appears at the door, with his dad close behind. "I'm here. What's going on?"

"We're going to look for Sadie," I tell him. "She's not at home."

His eyes widen with real panic. "Where the fuck is she?"

His reaction seems strong, but he's in charge of keeping her safe during the day. That must be why he's so worried.

"I don't know," I tell him honestly. "That's why we're going to look for her."

Micah's already turned and halfway out the door before I even finish the sentence.

"Be careful," my dad calls out after us, his voice echoing down the halls as we run to the door. Just before I go out, I grab the gun I keep by the front door. I have one at every door, just in case the wolf who killed my mother and sister ever comes back.

"Where would she go?" Micah growls as we get outside. "In the middle of the fucking night?"

Once again, I don't have the answer but I tell him what I do know. "Ava and Aaron must be with her. They're missing too."

Micah's eyes immediately glaze over, trying to reach out to them by mind-link. He frowns as his eyes clear. "I can't get through directly but I can hear some of Ava's thoughts. She's thinking about noise in the trees. They must be in the woods."

That helps a little, but we still need to narrow it down.

I need to think.

"Sadie doesn't have her wolf," I say, thinking it through out loud. "So they probably went down one of the paths. And the closest one to their house..."

"Is the one to the lake," Micah cuts me off as he runs forward and shifts into his wolf.

"Wait for me," I order him since he looks like he's about to take off without me. He growls in frustration but holds back, keeping pace with me as I take off at a sprint.

It's not too long before we come across an abandoned bike and Micah immediately sniffs at it before following his nose further into the woods.

It's frustrating as hell that I can't do all this stuff myself. I've always been looking forward to getting my wolf, but now I want him more than ever.

I cock the gun as we move deeper into the woods, just in case. Micah's ears are twitching more which I think must mean we're getting closer, and then we hear it.

A scream.

Sadie's scream.

~~**Sadie's PoV**~~

It's official. My life is completely insane.

A month ago, I was hanging out with my friends, going to school, arguing with my parents, just like any 17-year-old. Now, I'm sitting in the middle of a forest in the middle of the night with two wolves beside me, who also happen to be my cousins, hiding from some other wolves who might want to attack us for reasons that no one can seem to explain to me.

It's so ridiculous I want to laugh, but I hear something that makes the laughter die in my throat.

It's the sound of feet hitting the ground, running through the forest, fast.

No, not feet. *Paws.*

Ava's wolf turns to look at me and I nod back at her, understanding her silent instruction. *Keep quiet*, she's telling me.

For a minute, I think it worked. The sound seems to be getting quieter, like they've run right past us. But then it starts getting louder again, coming closer to us than it was before.

It's not quite as loud as it was the first time. Maybe just one or two wolves broke off from the others. But it gets closer and closer and closer until suddenly...

It stops.

I don't hear anything now. The ears on Ava and Aaron's wolves are twitching, straining for the sound too.

And then, out of nowhere, a wolf appears in front of us, and I scream.

I can't help it. It's like that moment in a horror movie where I would close my eyes, only now that it's actually happening to me, I can't look away.

All three wolves in front of me, Ava and Aaron and the unknown wolf, all wince, as if the sound hurts their ears. Maybe it does. Dogs have sensitive hearing, so I guess wolves are the same? I don't know why I'm thinking about this now. Do people always think about stupid things when their lives are in danger?

In any case, the wolves' disorientation only lasts a second before the new wolf growls, bares his teeth and charges straight at me.

Again, I can't look away. I see Aaron's wolf move in front of me to protect me, but before anything can happen, before the other wolf can reach either of us, yet another wolf hits him hard from the side. The two wolves roll around on the ground, teeth and claws bared, snarling and swiping at each other.

How is this my life?

"Sadie?" A worried voice calls out from the darkness and I tear my eyes away from the fight in front of me just as Aaron's wolf goes over to help.

"Logan?"

As soon as I say his name, he appears from the trees, dressed in only loose-fitting cotton pants and sneakers. He's holding a gun, his face grim, but when he sees me, relief crosses his face.

"Are you okay?" He hurries over to me, his hands brushing my face and my shoulders, looking for injuries.

"I'm fine," I tell him, trying to ignore that weird tingling feeling that starts up as soon as he touches me again. "But Aaron and the other wolf..."

Logan turns before I get the words out and I peer around him so I can see what's going on too.

It looks like Aaron and the wolf who just arrived have got the other wolf pinned down, so Logan walks over, holding the gun confidently as he takes aim at the intruder wolf.

I know it's not really appropriate given the circumstances, but I can't help thinking that he looks really fucking sexy right now.

"Shift," he orders, pointing the gun at the wolf. "Or there's a silver bullet with your name on it."

A silver bullet? I sort of remember hearing that werewolves don't like silver, back when I thought they weren't real. I guess that's something I should know, if I'm going to be one.

The wolf resists for a second, and Logan cocks the gun, his aim steady. "Last chance."

I could almost swear the wolf rolls his eyes, and a second later he starts turning into a man I've never seen before. A man who is completely naked.

Why is this not weird to anyone else?!

"Link the rest of the team, get them over here," Logan commands the wolf who's not Aaron before addressing the unknown man. "How many of you are there?"

"It's just me," the man says, his eyes fixed on Logan.

"That's a lie," I blurt out. Logan doesn't turn, keeping his eyes on the man, but I know he's listening to me. "I heard them running past. There was definitely more than one."

The man's eyes narrow as he looks over at me and he gives me a sinister grin. "Even if they don't get you tonight, sweetheart, someone will eventually. There's a bounty on your head so big that no rogue will pass it up."

Bounty? Rogue? What is he talking about?

Before I can ask, Logan looks at the other wolf. "Micah, shut him up."

Micah? The wolf is Micah? What is going on?

Once again, I don't get to ask the question out loud before the wolf sinks his sharp teeth into the man's leg, making him cry out in pain. "You fucking bastard!"

The sound of more wolves approaching fills the air, and I instinctively move closer to Logan.

"Don't worry, Sadie," he reassures me, putting a warm hand on my shoulder. "They're with us."

I don't know how he knows that, but sure enough, when they arrive, they don't attack. Two of the wolves transform into big, muscled men and they pick up the man with the bleeding leg between them and drag him away.

A third wolf changes to a man as well, and he goes up and speaks to Logan quietly for a moment before changing back to a wolf and leading all the others away.

"What's going on?" I ask, feeling completely out of the loop.

"They've already got the rest of them," Logan tells me, and I let out a sigh of relief. "It's safe now. Come on, let's get you home."

~~Micah's PoV~~

The way that Sadie is looking at Logan is making me feel a little sick. She's acting like he's the hero when I was the one that did all the work! I tracked her down and I stopped the wolf from attacking, but he's the one with the gun and the one that can speak to her, so he gets all the credit.

As usual, my contributions count for nothing.

We all start walking back towards the Millers' house, me and the twins still in our wolf forms, when Logan turns to me. "Micah, we're okay without you. Why don't you head back to the pack house and see what you can find out?"

I'm torn between being flattered that he wants me to take his place at the pack house and annoyed that he's sending me away from Sadie. She's still my responsibility, but he's my future Alpha, so I obey as graciously as I can. I try to catch Sadie's eye before I go, but she's only paying attention to Logan, and that strange, slightly nauseated feeling passes over me again.

When I get back to the pack house, I shift and grab a spare pair of pants from the stack by the door before heading to the Alpha's office. It's still buzzing with activity like it was earlier, but at least everyone is less tense now that the immediate danger is past.

"Micah," the Alpha greets me as I come in, and I feel a little pride that he's taken the time to address me personally. "Where's Logan?"

Oh. That's why he's paying attention to me: he just wants to know about his son. The pride drops like a weight in my stomach.

"He's helping Sadie get home," I answer, trying to stay professional.

"And she's okay?" he follows up.

"Yeah, but the wolf we captured, he said there would be others coming for her. He said there's a big bounty on her head and a lot of rogues want to claim it."

That gets his attention and everyone else in the room too. Suddenly, all eyes are on me.

"He was here for Sadie?" the Alpha asks me, his eyes focused intently on me.

I didn't realize they didn't already know that, but I nod confidently. "He spoke right to her. He seemed to know who she was."

"Come sit down," the Alpha invites me and I go to sit across from him just as I've seen my father do so many times before. "You've spent a lot of time with her this week. Have you noticed anything unusual about her?"

"Unusual?" I repeat, not quite sure what he's getting at. I've noticed plenty of things about her. The way she tucks her hair behind her ears when she's concentrating. The way she rolls her eyes when someone says something stupid and she thinks no one's watching. The way she puts her hand over her mouth when she thinks something's funny, probably because she doesn't like her laugh. That's my guess, anyway.

Or the way she makes me feel when she smiles at me. It's only happened once or twice, but it was a good feeling. I liked it.

I've decided that my initial weird feelings towards her were simply because she was something forbidden. My family would never accept the idea of me with a half-human girl, so it made the whole idea of her kind of exotic and a bit dirty, like some kind of strange fetish.

But now that I've gotten to know her a little bit, it's different. She still turns me on, I have to admit, but it's not for the same reason. Half the time I forget that she's only half wolf at all.

Sometimes, she's just Sadie.

But I don't think any of that is what the Alpha means about noticing things, and he quickly confirms I'm right.

"Any kind of signs of something different about her?" he asks me. "Any strange things happening when she's around? I'm just trying to figure out why anyone's interested in her at all."

I bite back the reply on the tip of my tongue, which is that there are lots of reasons why people would be interested in her. Again, I know that's not what he means.

"I haven't noticed anything like that, Alpha. She seems like a normal girl."

The Alpha sighs as he nods. "That's what I thought too. But if you do notice anything, let me know."

"Of course, sir."

He's about to dismiss me when my dad walks in and everyone in the room turns to him. His eyebrows raise a little when he sees me sitting across from the Alpha, but he ignores me to address his superior.

"I've completed the initial questioning, Alpha. They're all giving pretty much the same story as the wolf we caught earlier this week. Someone, but they don't know who, hired them to kill the half-breed, with a bonus for the wolf who succeeds."

"Sadie." My growl takes everyone in the room by surprise, but my dad most of all. He turns to me with a stern look of disapproval.

"What did you say?" he asks icily, daring me to repeat myself.

He expects me to back down, but I'm an adult now. I answer to my Alpha, not to him. "Her name is Sadie. It's not hard to remember."

The tension in the air is thick as my dad and I glare at each other, neither of us willing to look away first.

Finally, the Alpha clears his throat. "Thank you, Beta. Micah had already told us the same thing about the intruders, but it's good to have the confirmation."

My dad is taken aback by that and I can't help feeling a bit smug. He didn't expect me to have the information before he did.

But my smugness is short-lived because the Alpha dismisses me in the next breath. "You can go home now, Micah."

I don't want to go. I want to stay and help figure out what's happening, but there's nothing I can do but bow my head in submission.

As I get up to go, the Alpha calls out one more thing after me.

"Good work tonight, by the way. You're well on your way to being a key part of the team."

That's enough to send me out of the office with a smile.

Chapter Eleven

~~Logan's PoV~~

After Micah leaves, I turn back to Sadie. "Are you okay?"

I don't mean physically this time. I mean how she's feeling about the fact that a wolf just tried to kill her, and I know immediately that she understands me.

"What was that guy talking about?" she asks, glancing over at me before looking back at the path in front of us. "He said there's a bounty on me? And what's a rogue?"

"I have no idea what he was talking about with the bounty," I tell her truthfully. "But I think you should know that he's not the first one who came looking for you. The wolf in the school earlier this week was after you too."

I don't tell her to scare her, I just think it's better that she knows. I believe it's almost always better to be honest with people. After all, she probably wouldn't have gone out into the woods in the middle of the night if she knew people were after her. I don't want to think about how close she was to being injured, or worse.

"They want to kill me?" she asks, looking genuinely shocked. "Why? Because I'm half-human?"

Where did she get that idea?

As soon as I ask myself the question, I know the answer, and I could kill Micah for putting those kinds of thoughts in her head. "No, I don't think that's it. Most wolves don't care about that these days, there are just a few racist assholes left over who do."

Maybe I shouldn't call my best friend an asshole, but I'd say it to his face too if he were here.

"I don't know why they're after you," I continue. "But I'm going to figure it out. I won't let anything bad happen to you."

Her cheeks turn a bit red beneath the moonlight, and I realize what that sounded like.

"I mean, as the next Alpha, the whole pack's safety is my responsibility," I explain further, and I want to kick myself as the smile falls off her face.

Fuck, I'm making a mess of this.

"What about the other thing?" she asks, thankfully changing the subject. "What's a rogue?"

That's an easier question to answer. "Rogues are wolves without a pack. Usually, they've been kicked out of a pack for some reason and it's hard for werewolves to survive without a pack. It can make them desperate. So, sometimes people will hire rogues to do things they don't want to do themselves since they don't have any loyalty to anyone."

"And they're disposable," Sadie guesses. When I nod, her nose wrinkles in disgust. "How can you judge someone just by what pack they're in or if they're in a pack at all? Isn't that racist too? After all, they're people as well."

I know she's got a point. I'm sure not all rogues are bad, but we're taught to believe they are. I try to explain it better. "As I said, they've been kicked out of a pack for some reason, and it's usually because they did something pretty bad. So I guess you can kind of think of them like criminals. They're not all bad people, but you're going to be a bit more careful around them anyway."

"Will you guys kill those wolves who came here tonight?" she challenges me. I can tell she doesn't like the idea.

"They wanted to kill you," I remind her, not sure why she's so indignant on their behalf.

"That doesn't answer my question."

She's not backing down, so I answer her as honestly as I can. There's no point lying about it. "They'll be questioned for more information. After that, it's up to the Alpha what to do with them."

"And he might have them killed?" she presses.

"Yeah, he might."

There's silence for a few moments as she processes that. "What would you do in this situation when you're Alpha?"

Damn, she asks hard questions, but again, I have to be honest. "If they tried to kill you, I'd probably have them killed."

She goes quiet after that, but I don't know if I've upset her or not.

In another minute or two, we reach the edge of the forest and Aaron's wolf nudges my hand. When I look down at him, he gestures towards some clothes on the ground, and I realize this must be where they shifted. I nod at him to tell him I understand, and Sadie and I stand to the side while Aaron and Ava shift back and get dressed.

"Does that not seem weird to you?" Sadie asks, breaking her silence. I think she's still talking about the rogues, but then she gestures behind me. "The fact that your friends are naked right now?"

It's such an unexpected question that I laugh. That's twice in one day she's made me laugh. Twice more than I have in a very long time.

"You get used to it," I reply drily. "I promise."

The four of us walk the rest of the way together until we get back to the Millers' house. Rory Flanagan is standing outside the house, looking shame-faced. "Logan," he greets me respectfully, but he doesn't meet my eye. "I'm sorry."

I don't know what he's apologizing for, but Ava jumps in. "No, it's my fault, Rory. I distracted you so Sadie could sneak out. I'm sorry, that wasn't fair to you. I didn't mean to put anyone in danger."

Oh, that's what's going on. I put on my Alpha voice to address them. "You both should know better. Luckily, there was no harm done. Rory, you can stay at your post until you're relieved."

He nods and bows his head to me and we walk up to the house where Mr and Mrs Miller are waiting at the front door. They hug their kids and Sadie, but I can tell by the looks on their faces that all three of them are in for a lecture once I leave.

"Can I talk to Sadie for one more minute?" I ask them, and they immediately agree, going inside and leaving Sadie and I alone on the porch.

Even though we were kind of alone on the walk back, this is the first time we've really been alone tonight. She seems to realize it too, looking a bit more shy with me all of a sudden.

"I meant what I said about not letting anything bad happen to you," I tell her, and this time, she meets my eye. Her dark chocolate eyes shine beneath the porch lights. "I'm going to find out why they're after you. If you'd like to help me, you can."

"How could I help?" Sadie asks, sounding intrigued.

"I don't know yet," I admit. "But I'd like your input. Why don't you come to the pack house in the morning and we can sit down and review everything we know so far?"

She bites her lip and nods in agreement. I can't stop my eyes from going to her lips and just like at the gun range, I start to think about kissing her. Almost before I realize what I'm doing, I lean towards her, and she leans into me too.

Our faces are only inches apart when I suddenly remember that Rory is on the sidewalk, and her aunt and uncle are just inside, and we've really got more important things to be worried about right now. So at the last second, I change course and kiss her on the cheek instead.

"Have a good night, Sadie. And stay inside, okay?"

I give her a smile and she smiles back, but there might be a little bit of disappointment in it.

I kind of think she wanted to kiss me too.

The thought keeps me smiling as I head back home.

~~Sadie's PoV~~

As soon as I open my eyes the next morning, a million thoughts are already flying through my head. Between Ava and Aaron's party, our moonlit excursion out in the woods, and the fact that apparently someone out there wants me dead, I've got a lot to think about.

But one thing keeps pushing its way to the front of my brain, drowning out everything else.

Logan.

He almost kissed me last night. I thought for sure he was going to until at the last minute he seemed to change his mind and kissed my cheek instead. But even that little contact was enough to start my heart racing. As he walked away, my cheek felt warm where his lips had been, almost like I could still feel them there.

Not even my aunt and uncle's stern reprimands when I got back inside the house could wipe the smile off my face.

I've dated other boys before. I've fooled around with some of them too, but I haven't gone all the way yet. I'm not sure exactly what I'm waiting for, but I figure I'll know it when I feel it.

And the way I feel around Logan, well, that might be it. It's something new, anyway. He's not like anyone else I've ever met.

It's not that he's gorgeous. Okay, it's not *just* that he's gorgeous. I also like the way he talks to me straight, answers my questions and shares things with me. He's smart and he listens and he cares about people. I feel like we're really connecting.

But then there's still the fact that he's a werewolf! And not just any werewolf, but the one who will be in charge of this whole pack one day.

And I can tell from the things he's told me that he believes in all of this mate business and everything that goes with it.

Was that why he didn't kiss me last night when it seemed pretty clear he wanted to? Because I'm not his 'mate'?

It still strikes me as ridiculous. If we like each other, we should be able to decide to see each other. It shouldn't depend on what some goddess, who I'm not even sure exists, decides for us.

I shake my head at myself as I get in the shower. Why am I getting all worked up? I don't even know for sure that he does like me or if he really was thinking about kissing me. I'm getting way ahead of myself.

All I really know is that he invited me over to his house this morning and I'm planning on going.

It's not until I get out of the shower and get dressed that I realize I haven't even thought about my parents yet today. For the last two weeks they've been the first thing I think of as soon as I wake up, and today, they didn't even cross my mind until now. It makes me feel a bit guilty, but I think maybe it's a good thing too.

I'm finally starting to feel a bit more like myself again.

Ava and Aaron are both supposed to stay at home all day as their punishment for going out last night, but I think it's more because my aunt just wants to keep an eye on them and make sure they're both doing okay after everything that happened at the party. My aunt and uncle never specifically said that the restriction applied to me too, and sure enough, when I ask at breakfast if I can go to the pack house to see Logan, my aunt quickly agrees.

"Of course, Sadie," she smiles. "The Alpha's son wouldn't ask you over unless it was important."

I manage to stop myself from rolling my eyes. So Logan could do whatever he wanted and it would be okay because he's the Alpha's son? With that kind of attitude among the rest of the pack, it's amazing he's not a self-entitled asshole. Maybe his personality got switched with Micah somehow?

I send Logan a text to see what time he wants me to come over and he replies saying whenever I want, so I head out right away. The man watching our house, a different guy from the night before, follows behind me as I make my way through town. Even though I understand a little better now why I need a bodyguard, I still don't like it.

This is the first time I've gone to the pack house by myself and I'm not sure if I'm supposed to say something to the man who stands guard outside the door. Logan just nodded at him when he brought me here yesterday, but it's his house. So, I stop and say good morning and we talk for a minute before I ask if I can go in.

He gives me an amused smile. "The pack house belongs to the whole pack. You can go in whenever you like."

Oh. I didn't realize that. Isn't that weird for Logan that people can just go in and out of his house all the time? I don't think I would like it.

When I step inside the front hall, there's no one around and I'm not sure where to go next. There are four different hallways off the rectangular room, one to the left, one to the right, and one on either side of the big staircase that leads up to the next floor. I pull out my phone to send Logan another text when a voice calls out to me.

"Hey, Sadie."

I look up to see Micah standing in one of the doorways. He's not wearing his usual scowl that he has for me. In fact, he's almost smiling.

"Did you get back to sleep last night?"

The question throws me off until I remember that he was also there in the woods, as a wolf. Although I don't feel like I saw him, he obviously saw me.

"For a little bit," I answer vaguely. "What are you doing here?"

He winces a bit at my tone, and honestly, I didn't mean it to sound quite the way it came out. It's just the way I'm used to talking to him. It's kind of our thing.

"Logan asked me to come over and brainstorm with you guys," he replies.

Really? I can't help feeling a bit disappointed. I kind of hoped that Logan asking me over to talk about what happened was just an excuse to spend time with me, but I guess not.

"I don't know where to go," I admit, gesturing to all the different halls.

Micah smiles properly this time. "No problem. I'll show you."

He gestures down the hallway he's standing in, so I go over to him and we walk side-by-side down the hall. He stops in front of a door and I'm about to open it when he puts a hand on my arm.

"Listen, Sadie, before we go in, there's something I need to say."

I look up at him warily. I haven't liked most of what he's had to say to me before, but I let him speak.

"I'm sorry for the way I've been acting," he starts, and I blink in shock. Is Micah actually apologizing to me? That might be the most surprising thing that's happened since I got here, and that's saying something.

"I've never really spent time with any humans before," he continues, almost looking embarrassed. "I was told my whole life that they're not as good as us and I never bothered to question it. I guess it was kind of stupid. I should have made my own mind up instead of just believing what I was told."

That's actually a big deal for him to say that, I can tell. And he's changing his mind about all of humanity because of me? I'm kind of flattered.

"Well, I'm only half-human," I remind him. "So maybe I'm only half-bad."

He looks surprised and for a second I think he doesn't know I'm joking, but then he grins, and I remember how good-looking I thought he was the first time I saw him. When he's not being a total jerk, I can kind of see it again.

"Let's go with that," he agrees. He finally sounds friendly talking to me, like he does with other people. "After all, half-bad is still pretty good."

He opens the door and walks in, leaving me shaking my head in surprise in the whole exchange. Who'd have thought? Maybe there's a decent guy in there somewhere after all.

~~**Logan's PoV**~~

Micah comes into my office with Sadie just behind him and I greet them both and get right down to business. "I know my dad's got his own team looking into this, but the more ideas we have, the better. The three of us are pretty smart and obviously, Sadie, you'll know your own past better than anyone. Let's figure out why someone wants you dead."

They both agree and we dive in. I've made a list of questions for Sadie about what her life was like before she came to Westbridge, but as she answers them, nothing stands out to me. We already knew that she didn't know about werewolves. She's certain she's never been to any other packs besides ours. Her parents never mentioned any kind of enemies or dangerous people they knew.

There's something else I want to ask her and I don't know if it will upset her. The last thing I want to do is make her feel worse, but I think it's an important question. It's been bugging me for a little while now, so finally, I just spit it out.

"Do you think there's any chance that your parents' accident wasn't an accident at all?"

As I expected, she looks shocked at the suggestion. "What do you mean? It was snowing and the road was icy. That's what the police said."

I nod as supportively as I can. "I know. But was there anything at all that seemed strange about it to you? Even just a little thing?"

She pauses to think while Micah and I wait patiently. "Well, my dad was always a really careful driver," she says slowly. "If there was any kind of bad weather, he'd usually pull over and wait it out. It's a bit weird that he would have kept going if the roads were really that bad."

"Good." That was exactly the kind of thing I was talking about. "Anything else?"

"I heard one of the policemen say that the tires on the car were worn, but they shouldn't have been," she adds, getting a little more worked up. "He just had them replaced a few weeks before. I know because I went with him to get it done."

I can see her getting more agitated as she thinks about it, and when she looks back at me, there's dismay on her face.

"Do you think someone messed with their car on purpose?"

I recognize the pain in her voice and my chest tightens. I wish I could make her feel better, but I know there's nothing I can say. If it's true, she's going to have to learn to live with it. "I don't know for sure, but it's possible. Where were your parents going when the accident happened?"

"To visit some friends. I was supposed to go too, but I had a school assignment that I needed to finish, so I convinced them to let me stay home."

That uneasy feeling in the back of my brain gets stronger. "You should have been in the car too?"

She nods, and I see the guilt in her face, the same guilt I've lived with for the last year.

The guilt of surviving.

It's just about the worst feeling I can think of.

But what she's just said makes me even more convinced that I'm right. These attempts to kill her didn't just start when she got to Westbridge. I think someone wanted to kill her in that car, that she was a target even then. Were they trying to kill her parents too, or were they just in the wrong place at the wrong time? That's one of the things I don't know yet.

"Micah, we should get a copy of the police report and anything we can find about the car itself."

He's already making notes. "Got it."

Even if I am right, it still doesn't answer the big questions though. Who's behind this, and why Sadie?

Micah jumps in to talk about just that. "These rogues keep saying they've been hired by someone to kill Sadie, right?"

I nod.

"So, why don't we send someone undercover? Have them pose as a rogue who just got kicked out of the pack and is looking for work? I bet whoever it is would jump at the chance to hire someone who really knows the pack territory, and then our guy could try to find out who it is."

That's a really smart idea. I don't have the authority to plan anything like that though, so we need to take it to someone who does. "I think you should suggest it to my dad."

I get up and knock on the door that connects my office to my dad's. He calls out for me to come in and I open it to find him with his own team of advisors, reviewing not only last night's attack but the mate issue as well.

I bring Sadie and Micah in and Micah repeats the suggestion he made to me. I can see my dad is impressed, like I knew he would be, but Micah's dad quickly jumps in to shoot down the idea.

"It would be too suspicious, Alpha." His tone is completely dismissive. "They'd immediately suspect that it was a setup and it would endanger not only the wolf who took on such a foolish mission, but it could further endanger Ms Jennings too if they realize that we're onto them. It could make them more desperate. We need to actually be smart about this, not jump on the first thing that comes into our heads."

Micah's fists clench at his sides though he tries to keep his face neutral, and I don't blame him for being upset. I still think it's a clever idea and not foolish at all. And even if it wasn't, there are kinder ways of disagreeing with it.

"We'll consider it," my dad says to Micah, giving him a more supportive look than his own father does. "I appreciate that you're putting some thought into this."

That's obviously a dismissal, so the three of us return back to my office and Sadie gives Micah a sympathetic look. "Is your dad always that much of a jerk?"

Micah and I look at each other in surprise before we both laugh. A lot of people might think that about the Beta, but not everyone would say it out loud, especially to his son.

But Sadie's not like everyone else. I already know that.

Micah nods at her as his laughter trails off. "Yeah, pretty much. That's just how he is."

"Well, I thought it was a good idea," she says, and I can see Micah stand a little taller at that.

"Me too," I agree. "A really good idea."

The more I think about it, the more I like it, actually. The quickest way of figuring all of this out will be going straight to the source. But because the idea came from Micah, I know Beta Aldric will fight it every step of the way, and we can't afford to waste any more time. They've already tried to kill Sadie twice in the last week. Who knows what they might try next?

"And if the Alpha council isn't going to take it seriously, maybe we should look into it on our own," I suggest.

Both of them look at me curiously. "What do you mean?" Sadie asks.

"I mean that we've already got someone who could do the job," I reply. "Someone who everyone already knows doesn't get along with his dad. Someone who might consider leaving the pack and trying to make it on his own?"

Micah's eyes widen with both surprise and excitement. "Me? You think I could do it?"

"If you want to," I clarify. "I think it's worth a shot. What do you say, Micah? Feel like going rogue?"

Chapter Twelve

~~**Micah's PoV**~~

The next week goes incredibly quickly. I can't remember ever feeling as excited about anything as I do about the secret mission that Logan, Sadie and I are working on. Finally, I'm going to prove to everyone exactly what I can do.

Logan thinks that if we try to go through his dad, my dad will find a way to block us, and I can't really argue with that. While Logan's dad is including him more in the pack management day-to-day, especially now that's about to turn 18, mine is still determined to keep his own iron grip over all the Beta's duties.

It's like he sees me as a threat to his power rather than his successor that he should be training. I don't understand it at all.

But Logan argues that we don't need their support to go ahead with our plan, and once again, I agree. The fewer people that know about it, the better. It will be more convincing that I really have gone rogue if the Alpha and his whole team are surprised by it. And Logan assures me that the Alpha will restore my link to the pack as soon as I'm finished. He says he'll take any blame for the mission that might come down on us from the pack leadership.

He's a good friend and I'm so glad he's acting more like his old self. Sadie seems to have had a good influence on both of us.

The three of us have spent a lot of time together this week. During school, I'm still watching out for Sadie like before, and ever since I apologized to her, she doesn't seem to mind me being around so much. We talk and joke around with each other, and it's nice. She's a bit sarcastic a lot of the time but not in a nasty way. She makes me laugh.

After school, we go to the pack house and make plans with Logan. I wanted to run out and get started as soon as we came up with the plan on Sunday, but he's insisting that we make backup plans, and backup plans for the backup plans. He wants to make sure that nothing goes wrong, and I respect that. I know he still feels responsible for what happened to Kara and the Luna, and I know he would blame himself if something happened to me too. So, for his sake as much as for my own, I'm taking it all very seriously. I won't do anything reckless.

"What do you do if someone gets suspicious about why you left Westbridge?" he quizzes me on Friday. We've been over this every day this week, and I know that he knows I know the answer, so I decide to have a little fun with him.

"I tell them that the Alpha's decided to turn the whole pack vegan and I couldn't take it anymore. I just really needed a hamburger."

Sadie laughs while Logan scowls at me. "You need to focus, Micah."

"Oh, come on, Mr Alpha-in-training," Sadie says, giving him a playful shove. "You know he's got this."

She gives me a supportive smile that makes my whole body feel lighter. Nobody's ever looked at me like that, like they have total faith in me.

How did I go from thinking she was worthless two weeks ago to having her opinion mean more to me than anyone else's? I don't really get it, but it feels so good, I'm not going to question it.

"I *am* focused," I tell Logan. "I'm doing this for Sadie. I won't mess up."

I look back over at her to show her I mean it, and she blushes a little bit before looking down. She does that every time I try to show her that I care about her, and I don't know what it means.

Logan relents. "I know you won't. Sorry. It's just important to me that this all goes well. For all of us."

"I know."

We nod at each other in understanding, and Logan leans back in his chair with a sigh. "You know what, we've probably been doing this long enough. Why don't we take tonight off?"

Really? Our plan is to leave first thing in the morning, so I was sure he'd want to keep going over things until the last minute. But Sadie's right, I *do* have this. I know everything inside and out and I feel totally prepared. A night off sounds like a much better idea.

Especially if I get to spend it with Sadie. I'm about to open my mouth to ask her if she wants to do something, but she speaks before I get a chance.

"We should watch a movie," she suggests, looking between me and Logan. "Something totally brainless."

I can't help feeling a little disappointed that she's included Logan in this. I was kind of hoping to spend time with her alone.

But he nods in agreement, so I have no choice but to do the same. "What do you want to watch?"

"How about Twilight?" she suggests mischievously, laughing when Logan and I both immediately cry out, "No!"

"Anything but that," I plead.

We settle on an action film and agree to meet back here at the pack house after dinner. I walk Sadie to her aunt and uncle's house, trying to figure out how to tell her how I'm feeling before I have to leave tomorrow. I have no idea how long I'm going to be gone for, and just in case anything does happen to me, I don't want to miss my chance.

I've never been nervous with a girl like this before. But just when I think I'm ready to say something, we get to her house, and she turns to me with a smile. "Thanks, Micah. I'll have Ava or Aaron walk me over to the pack house after we eat, so you can just meet me there. See you later!"

She's gone before I even have a chance to open my mouth.

~~Aaron's PoV~~

Sadie comes in just as we're all sitting down to dinner. She's in a good mood, just like she has been most of the week, but she's the only one in the house who is. It's like a complete role reversal from the week before, when she was still feeling down and uncomfortable about being new here and we were all trying to cheer her up. Now, she's the one trying to lift our spirits.

"Did you hear anything at the pack house?" Ava asks her when we're all settled at the table. "Have they figured out what's going on yet?"

Ava's wolf is still bugging her every day, hounding her to go and claim her mate. It's wearing my sister down, and I feel bad for her, and for Laurel too. She hardly wanted to see me all week, she says she can't handle her wolf arguing with her either.

Sadie shakes her head apologetically. "No, they haven't heard anything."

As promised, the Alpha made his announcement on Sunday to the whole pack that something had gone wrong with the mate bonds, not only here but in the neighboring packs as well, and that until they were sure it was fixed, all mating claims should be put on hold. Of course it was our classmates that were most upset about it, the ones, like us, who were just turning 18 and were eager to find their mates. Someone asked how long the Alpha expected the hold to last, but he couldn't say.

Now, we're just in limbo. At least my wolf hadn't recognized the wrong mate, or any mate at all, so I don't have to deal with what Ava and Laurel are going through, but it's still hard for me.

I miss my girlfriend. It feels like half of me is missing.

When we finish eating, Sadie asks me to walk her back to the pack house. She's been spending an awful lot of time there this week, but it seems to be making her happy, so no one's saying too much about it.

"You could come in too," she offers after she tells me she's just watching a movie tonight with Logan and Micah. "A little mindless distraction might be good for you."

I appreciate the offer, but I know I'm not good company right now. "No, it's okay. Thanks, but I'm just going to spend the night at home."

Sadie sighs with frustration. "Aaron, you've got to stop moping about this. Who cares whether some goddess made a mistake, or who she wanted you to be with in the first place? You know who you want to be with. You've always known. Just go be with her!"

I shake my head sadly. "It doesn't work that way, Sadie."

"It can," she argues. "You have a brain and a heart of your own, Aaron. You don't need anyone telling you what's right for you."

She gives me a slightly pitying look before she goes into the house, greeting the man on duty at the door by name.

I don't like her pity, and maybe she's got a point. Laurel and I love each other. We're both adults now. What's stopping us from being together if that's really what we want?

Before I know it, my feet are taking me to Laurel's house, and her face shows her surprise when she opens the door to find me there.

"Aaron, I thought we agreed that we would wait for the Alpha to…"

I don't let her finish. My arms go around her and I kiss her harder than I've ever kissed her before. I want to make any doubts she's feeling disappear.

She clings to me with a quiet desperation, like I'm the only thing keeping her afloat in a sea of uncertainty.

"Are your parents home?" I whisper, praying with every part of me that the answer's no, and when she shakes her head, I could almost cry with relief.

"They've gone to the city for the weekend," she says. "They wanted me to come too, but I was too upset."

Of course she was, but that ends now. I want to make her feel a million different things, but upset isn't one of them.

Before she can object, I pick her up, kick off my shoes, and carry her upstairs to her room. Her cheeks flush red as she realizes where we are and I place her down on her bed gently. "I don't care if you're my mate or not," I tell her, kissing her nose and her eyelids gently. "I love you, Laurel."

"I love you, too," she says, her eyes brimming with tears. I brush them away before kissing her eyelids again, making her laugh.

"I want to make love to you," I tell her. I've never wanted anything more. "If you want me to."

She nods, laughing and crying at the same time. "I want to, Aaron. I want to be with you."

Thank the goddess. Or screw the goddess, in this case. Right now, I couldn't care less about her. All that matters to me is the beautiful goddess of a woman right in front of me.

I help her take all her clothes off, and we take mine off together too. I've never seen her naked before and she's just as stunning as I could have imagined. She stares at me, her eyes and her hands running across my body as I kiss her again, my need for her growing with every second.

"Is your wolf freaking out at you?" I ask. I don't want to kill the mood, but I want to know everything about how she's feeling.

And to my relief, she shakes her head. "She knows this is what I want. She's not fighting me."

Good. I kiss her lips again, her neck and down her body to her beautiful breasts. When I take her stiff nipple into my mouth, she gasps and the sound sends a wave of pleasure through me.

"Aaron," she moans as her body writhes beneath me. "I need you. Please."

I was trying to take things slower, but the longing in her voice is more than I can take. I pull out the condom from the pocket of my jeans, the one I've been carrying around in anticipation of this very moment for weeks, and roll it on my hard cock without too much trouble. I'd practiced a few times at home to make sure I could do it, though I wasn't planning on telling her that.

"I don't really know what I'm doing," I tell Laurel honestly as she spreads her legs for me and I settle my hot and heavy cock at her entrance. "I don't want to hurt you."

"I don't care," she promises. "I just want to be yours, Aaron."

That's what I want too. So I push into her, as gently as I can, and it feels so good I almost come right then and there. She's tight and wet and warm and perfect.

"Deeper," she encourages me, so I obey, pushing into her harder until she whimpers in pain and I immediately freeze.

"Fuck, Laurel, I'm sorry."

She just shakes her head at me. "Don't be. I'm fine. Keep going."

Eventually, I'm all the way in and it's the best feeling in the whole damn world. I've never felt as connected to anyone as I do right now, and I know from the way she looks at me that she's feeling the same.

"You're mine, Laurel," I tell her, feeling a strange possessiveness inside me that I've never had before. "No one else's."

She nods. "Always."

I begin to move in her and it's a bit awkward at first, until suddenly, it's not, and then we're both calling out for each other and the world explodes around me as Laurel shudders in my arms.

Who needs the moon goddess, I wonder as I gradually drift back down to earth and into the arms of my lover. I have everything I need right here.

~~**Sadie's PoV**~~

Logan's already waiting for me when I get back to the pack house, and he gives me a warm smile when he sees me. He's smiling a lot more lately and it really suits him.

"Do you want to help me make some popcorn?" he asks as we walk together to the big kitchen where all the meals are prepared for everyone in the house. "I kind of suck at cooking."

"Making popcorn isn't exactly cooking," I point out with a laugh. "I don't think you can really do it wrong."

"Challenge accepted," he grins, and we both laugh as he pulls a popcorn popper out of the cupboard and goes in search of the kernels to get started.

This is the first time we've been alone together in almost a week, since that night in the woods where he dropped me back off at my house and kissed my cheek. We've been so busy since then and Micah's been with us all the time, so there hasn't been any chance to find out if he had actually wanted to kiss something other than my cheek that night.

He hasn't done anything since then to indicate that he sees me as anything other than a friend. He's friendly with me at school, but he's friendly with everyone else too. Everyone's really happy about how much he's changed in the last couple of weeks. Ava told me yesterday that it must be because of me, but I think that's an exaggeration. I think it has a lot more to do with him feeling like he's got a purpose again with all the things going on and the mission we're planning.

He finds the popcorn and brings it over, measuring some out into the popper, then switches it on while he looks for butter and garlic salt. I'm not so sure about the garlic salt, but he promises I'm going to love it.

Garlic isn't something you offer to someone you're planning to kiss later, I can't help thinking. I guess that's not something he has in mind.

When he's found everything, he comes back over and puts it all down on the counter while the popcorn kernels keep spinning around in the hot air popper. "I'm doing the right thing here, aren't I?" he asks me, looking really serious all of a sudden.

"With the popcorn?" I ask in confusion.

He smiles again, shaking his head. "No, sorry. I just mean with Micah, sending him out on his own. I feel pretty sure about it, but then I think if something goes wrong..."

The worry and the guilt in his voice tugs at my heart, and I put my hand on his on top of the counter to comfort him. "He knows the risks," I point out. "He's making the choice, and you've done everything you can to support him. There are always going to be things in life you can't control, especially if you're going to be in charge of this whole pack someday."

His lips tighten and that flash of pain runs through his eyes, the same one I've seen before. "I know that, but I've made the wrong choice before. I don't want to..."

I don't know what comes over me, but I'm so eager to get him to stop doubting himself, to make sure that not another word leaves his mouth, that I place my lips on his to shut him up.

Logan tenses in surprise, and for a second I think he's going to pull away from me. But he doesn't.

He kisses me back instead, sending little flickers of electricity running through my whole body. His hand cradles the back of my head as he pulls me a little bit closer, and I almost feel like I'm drowning. I need air, but I don't want it. I don't want him to stop.

His tongue runs gently along the seam of my lips and I open them just enough for his tongue to find mine, sending another cascade of little tingles down my spine. My arms go around his neck as his free hand grabs my waist and it's the best kiss I've ever had, without a doubt.

At least it is until I start to smell something burning.

Logan must smell it at the same time because he pulls back from me with wide eyes. "Oh, fuck!"

We both turn to where the popcorn maker is billowing out clouds of grey smoke. He frantically unplugs the machine while I grab the spray hose from the sink, dousing the overheated kernels before they can set off the fire alarm and send the whole house into a panic.

When the smoke clears, my eyes meet Logan's and we both burst out laughing.

"I told you I could ruin it," he manages to say, which only makes me laugh harder.

"How is that even possible?" I tease him.

He examines the machine and gives me a sheepish look. "I think I forgot to open up the chute for the popcorn to come out of."

That sets us off laughing again, which is when Micah walks in.

"What's so funny?" he asks, just as his nose starts twitching. "And what the fuck is that smell?"

Logan and I laugh harder, leaving Micah confused. "Let's just have some chips," Logan suggests, grabbing a bag from the cupboard and a bowl from the counter. "It's much safer."

With our snacks in place, the three of us head to the pack house lounge where there's a big screen TV and a bunch of comfy chairs and couches. I'm hoping that Logan will sit beside me, especially after that kiss we just shared, but he grabs one of the big chairs, so Micah and I follow suit, each of us in our own chair.

We all talk and make jokes through the movie, which is just what I wanted, something that doesn't require too much brain power to follow. Logan's as friendly to me as always, but he never quite meets my eye.

I hope that when the movie's over he'll ask me to stay a bit longer. I want to kiss him again, I can't deny that, but I also want to just talk to him about it. What is he thinking about what happened between us?

But when the credits finish rolling, he stands up and flicks on the lights. "We should all get some rest," he says, speaking to Micah more than me. "We've got an early start."

We're planning on taking a trip off the pack territory, the three of us, so it's not suspicious that Micah's leaving. Then once we're gone, he'll renounce his link to the pack. They both talk about it like it's something very dramatic, so I have to admit I'm curious to see what happens.

Micah nods. "I'll walk you home, Sadie."

I look over at Logan to see if he'll object to that, but he just nods. "Sounds good. See you both in the morning."

He walks away without another word.

"Everything okay?" Micah asks, watching me closely, and I realize I must have been frowning after Logan's retreating form.

"Fine," I lie. "Come on, let's go."

It's dark out, so Micah doesn't say much on the walk home since he's too busy keeping an eye out for trouble. He really does care about keeping me safe. He's a much better guy than he initially showed himself to be.

When we get to my house, I'm ready to say goodnight and head in, but he stops me. "Sadie, there's something I want to say to you before tomorrow. I don't know how things are going to go, and I think I'd regret it if I didn't say it."

I've never heard Micah sound like this before. He almost sounds nervous.

"Sure, go ahead," I tell him, trying to put him at ease.

He takes a deep breath. "I know I was a complete asshole to you when you got here, and I wouldn't blame you if you hate me."

Is that what he's worried about? "You already apologized to me," I reminded him. "And I've forgiven you. We're good, right? I thought we were good."

"We are," he quickly agrees. "But I just thought maybe... we could be something more than good?"

I don't understand. "What do you mean?"

He grimaces, like that wasn't the answer he was hoping for. "I mean, I like you Sadie. As more than a friend."

What? This is completely out of the blue. Have I been so focused on Logan that I've missed any signs Micah was giving me?

Before I can figure out what to say, he leans down and kisses me.

Chapter Thirteen

~~Logan's PoV~~

With a groan, I flop down on my bed. I've screwed up and now I don't know how to fix it.

After I almost kissed Sadie last weekend, I was feeling pretty good about the whole thing. It was nice to have something to be excited about again, and the thought of actually kissing her properly in the near future was definitely exciting.

But all it took was a few words from my dad to bring me back to reality.

He called me into his office on Sunday after Micah and Sadie left, after we'd secretly started planning the mission we were going to put in motion tomorrow. His team had all left too, so it was just me and him in the big room as he pulled out his bottle of scotch.

"You want some?" he asked.

I must have looked shocked because he laughed. "You're 18 in a couple of weeks, Logan. I think you can handle the odd drink. Besides, most kids your age are out getting drunk every weekend, right?"

I didn't think the Alpha was supposed to know about that, but it must have been the same when he was my age.

"Sure," I agreed cautiously. "I'll take some."

He poured me a small amount, less than half of what he took and handed it to me across the desk. We both raised our glasses silently, and I winced a little as the amber liquid burned my throat on the way down.

My dad laughed again. "You'll get used to that." A moment later, he sighed, looking tired and older all of a sudden. "Things are a real mess right now. Between this craziness with the mating bond and someone trying to kill one of my pack members... it's times like this when I really miss your mom."

I couldn't have been more surprised. He never talked to me about her, but maybe after the talk we'd had in the garden a few days ago, he felt we could be more open about it. I tried to encourage him to keep going. "What do you miss about her?"

He smiled through the sadness in his eyes. "Whenever something was going wrong, she used to come in here and have a drink with me. She'd let me rant away about whatever was bugging me, and then she'd do something that made it all seem better."

I didn't know exactly what he was talking about but I thought I could guess he meant something sexual, and he laughed again as he saw the discomfort on my face.

"Nothing like that," he said drily. "It was never any one particular thing. She just always knew exactly what I needed, just a few words or a hug, or whatever it might be. The mate bond is so special, Logan, finding that one person who completes you. If we lose it for good... I don't know what that means for us, as a pack, or even as a species. It's our greatest blessing, the best part of being a werewolf."

I had always felt the same but I knew that Sadie didn't agree, and to be honest, listening to her talk about it, I had started questioning whether she had a point. But hearing how strongly my dad felt, now I wasn't so sure anymore.

"I'm proud of you, you know, that you've waited to find your mate," he continued, looking over at me with an affectionate smile. "I promise I'll do everything I can to make sure that this bond mess is cleaned up before we get to your birthday."

I didn't feel I had anything to be proud of. I'd only avoided getting involved with anyone else because I was in mourning for the last year, and I just spent all of the night before thinking about getting involved with Sadie.

But maybe my dad was right. Maybe it *was* better to wait. It wasn't that much longer, and the last thing I would want to do was hurt Sadie if she didn't turn out to be my mate.

So, I decided after that conversation that I would back off a bit. I was still going to hang out with Sadie. We were friends now, not to mention she was involved in everything we were planning. But I wouldn't make any other kind of move, at least not yet.

I didn't count on *her* kissing *me*.

Standing in the kitchen with the popcorn maker whirring in the background, she kissed me, and it felt just as good as I could have imagined. Better, even. The same little tingles I'd felt earlier erupted on my lips as they connected with hers and I felt something I hadn't felt in a really long time.

I felt *hope*.

Unfortunately, we nearly burned the house down, and then Micah came in, and as things started to sink in, I realized that no matter how good it felt, it wasn't the right thing to do, not right now. So, I took the coward's way out and avoided her the rest of the night, and now, I'm lying on my bed feeling more conflicted than I have about anything in a long time.

I have to talk to her, that much is clear, but it's not going to be easy. I know she'll tell me it's a stupid reason not to pursue the obvious connection between us, but it's not just about me. It's about her too, plus I've got a responsibility to the pack. I have to set a good example, and falling for someone who might not be my mate isn't the way to do that.

I'll have to make Sadie understand. I just don't have any idea yet how I'm going to do that.

~~**Micah's PoV**~~

Sadie's eyes are wide as I pull back from her. It wasn't the best kiss ever, I have to admit. I knew after the way she'd reacted to what I said that she wasn't really expecting it and I didn't want to overdo it. But even so, it felt good to me. Her lips are as soft and sweet as I thought they'd be, and my whole body felt lighter as we were touching. I hope she feels the same.

"Micah, this is..." she trails off as she takes a small step back from me. "Really surprising. Two weeks ago, you hated me."

I wince, because she's right. I can't deny it. "Well, I was being stupid, like I already told you. I judged you before I got to know you. And now that I know you... I like you."

It shouldn't be so hard to say, but it still is. I've never told a girl I liked her before. I've told Blair, and a few of the other girls before her, that I liked certain *parts* of them, but never just that I liked them overall, as a person.

She's still looking surprised, so I keep talking. "Look, you don't need to say anything right now. I know I kind of sprung it on you, and I'm going away tomorrow anyway. I just wanted to let you know how I felt, and you can think about it while I'm gone."

Sadie nods slowly. "Okay. I will."

"Good." That's all I wanted, I try to tell myself, even though it's a lie. I wanted her to kiss me back and tell me she feels the same, but I guess it's too soon. I'm not going to push her. "I'll see you in the morning then. Good night, Sadie."

"Good night, Micah."

She gives me a small smile before going inside. I wait until I hear the door lock behind her before I head home.

In the morning, I'm up early. I've already got a backpack packed with a few clothes and essentials I'll need for my time away from the pack. It's really impossible to say how long it's going to take. Logan got some information from his dad's files about a bar in the city where rogues are known to hang out. He thinks I should start there.

I'm really excited as I head out to the pack house where Sadie and Logan are waiting for me. I know it's going to be dangerous, but that's okay. If I can help the pack, and help to protect Sadie, I'm willing to take the risk. That's what being a Beta is all about.

Logan smiles at me as I walk up. "You got everything?"

I nod. "I think so."

"Well, here's some extra cash, just in case," he says, shoving some bills into my hand. "And I got you a couple of burner phones so you can get in touch with me if you need to."

He hands those to me too and I shove one in my pocket and slip the other one into my bag. "Let's get going then."

Sadie smiles at both of us, but she's looking a bit uncomfortable. Is it because I kissed her last night, or is it because she's worried about me? I wish I could ask her, but it's not really possible with Logan right there.

We all get in his car and head out over the border crossing. Logan tells the guard on duty that we're all going out to the city for the day to visit some of Sadie's friends, and the guy doesn't question it. Why would he? It's not like the Alpha's son would lie to him.

And it's not totally a lie. We *do* plan to have a little fun first. It takes a few hours to get there, so we talk about school and our classmates and the mission, and anything except what I really want to talk about, which is how Sadie feels about last night. When we get to the city, Sadie shows us a few places she used to hang out and we all get something to eat before going to a park where we can find a quiet place where we won't be disturbed.

"Are you ready?" Logan asks me, and I nod with determination even though I'm a little scared now that the time has come.

I've always been part of the pack. I don't know what it's going to feel like to not be.

From my pocket, I pull out the switchblade I packed for the trip. It will come in handy for self-defense if I need it, but right now, I've got another use for it.

Flipping the blade open, I cut down the center of my palm. Sadie sucks in air through her teeth at the sight of it, but the pain isn't that bad. I turn my hand face down so the blood drips down onto the grass.

I speak out loud, clear and strong. "I, Micah Geary, hereby renounce my link to the Westbridge Pack and its Alpha."

Even though I warned my wolf it was coming, he still howls in anger in my head and my whole body feels numb, like a part of me has been cut off.

All three of us are silent for a minute, until Sadie speaks up. "Is that it?"

Logan and I look at each other in surprise and we both laugh. "It's kind of a big deal," he tells her, before looking back at me. "Try linking the pack."

I do, and there's nothing there. Just dead silence in my head.

"Good," he says. "I guess you're a rogue then."

Shit. I really am.

This is where they leave me. Logan and I shake hands, and I turn to Sadie, not sure what I should do with her, but she surprises me by giving me a hug. Her body is warm and soft against mine, and I don't want it to end.

"Be careful," she whispers in my ear. "I want you coming back safe and sound, ok?"

It's not quite a declaration of how she feels, but I'll take it. She cares about me at least a little. She doesn't want me to get hurt.

"I'll do my best," I promise, reluctantly letting her go as I look over at Logan. "I'll get in touch as soon as I've got something to share."

Logan nods and Sadie gives a wave as I grab my bag and head out into the city to find the other rogues.

~~Sadie's PoV~~

I'm still a bit confused about what I just witnessed as Logan and I walk back to the car. The way they were talking about breaking the link to the pack, I kind of expected thunder crashes and storm clouds to roll in, but I didn't actually see anything happen other than Micah grimace a little bit.

They both say it's a big deal so it must be a big deal, but I still don't get it.

What's a bigger deal to me is how Micah kissed me last night. I honestly hadn't thought about him in that way at all, mostly because he was such an ass to me when I first arrived. He's been nicer to me lately, but I figured it was just a matter of tolerating me now. I never guessed that he was actually interested in me like that.

And the kiss was kind of nice, I have to admit. He's a really good-looking guy; I thought that even when I thought he was an ass, but when he's relaxed and laughing, it makes him even better-looking. He makes me laugh too, and he makes me feel protected when he's watching out for me.

Is there a spark there? I really don't know. I thought about it for a long time last night. I don't feel naturally drawn to him like I do with Logan, like I did from the first time Logan and I met. But I like that Micah was up front with me and told me how he felt without putting any pressure on me to reciprocate. Especially since Logan seems to have withdrawn from me, and I don't know why.

However, we've got a long drive together back to Westbridge now, and I intend to find out.

"What's going on with you?" I ask him as soon as we're back out on the highway and he doesn't have to pay so much attention to the roads.

Logan's eyes dart over to me nervously. "What do you mean?"

"You know what I mean. We kissed in your kitchen last night and then you pretended it didn't happen. How is that supposed to make me feel?"

He winces as he takes one hand off the wheel to rub the back of his neck. "You're right, that was a shitty thing to do. I'm sorry."

Well, at least we agree on that. "So, what's going on? If you didn't like it, you can just tell me so, but it kinda felt to me like you did."

I've kissed enough guys to know when they're into it or not, and I'm pretty damn sure Logan was into it.

He winces again, his face scrunching up uncomfortably. "Of course I liked it. I like you, Sadie. I think that's obvious."

"It's not really obvious when you push me away like that." I wasn't letting him off the hook so easily.

"Okay, well, let me be clear. I like you, Sadie."

Warmth spreads through me as I hear the sincerity in his voice. He's not just saying that. He really does mean it, but that only leaves me more confused.

"What's the problem, then? In case it wasn't obvious, I like you too."

I thought kissing him was a pretty big hint in that direction, but maybe he needs to hear the words too.

He looks pleased that I've said it, a smile crossing his face, but a moment later, he sighs.

"The problem is that you might not be my mate."

I groan in frustration. "Are you kidding me?" After everything that's just happened with Ava and Aaron and Laurel, how is that possibly a valid excuse right now?

He sighs again at the question, but he doesn't back down. "I'm serious. My dad and I had a talk, about the whole mess with mates and why it's such a big deal. I know you don't understand it, Sadie, but it really is a vital part of who we are as werewolves. Your mate is the ideal person for you. We can't choose any better than the moon goddess chooses for us."

"You can't really believe that." He's so enlightened about everything else, how can he hold to that kind of idea? "How is some goddess supposed to know better than you who's right for you? How do you even know she's real? Has anyone ever seen her?"

"Yeah, actually, they have."

His answer takes me completely by surprise. I wasn't expecting that and my shock shows in my voice. "Really?"

Logan laughs at the change in my tone. "Yeah. I haven't seen her personally, but other people have. Apparently, because there are so many wolves all over the world, she doesn't have time to watch over them all at the same time, so she chooses representatives in different packs, kind of like delegates, to hold some of her power."

"What kind of powers do they have?" This all sounds like science fiction to me, but Logan obviously believes it, so I try to as well.

"They don't actually get powers of their own. It's more like they're vessels for the moon goddess' wishes. Her plans flow through them, if that makes sense. Her presence in them helps to keep everything running smoothly."

It doesn't completely make sense to me, but it does make me wonder. "What would happen if something happened to these vessels? Like, if they die?"

Logan frowns. "I think she chooses a new one before that happens."

"But what if she didn't?" I press, starting to get excited as the idea comes together in my head. If he's telling me the truth, then I might be onto something. "Wouldn't that mean her plans got messed up? Like, maybe with people getting the wrong mates?"

Logan immediately understands what I'm saying and his eyes go wide. "Holy shit. You might be right, Sadie. Maybe that's what's going on. Maybe something happened to the person who was the moon goddess' vessel. I have to tell my dad, hang on."

He starts punching in a number on the car's computer and soon, he's got the Alpha on his phone, filling him in on what I've just said.

The Alpha's deep voice comes through the car speakers. "That's very clever, Sadie, well done. I can't believe none of us thought of it."

I'm a bit surprised too. I mean, I barely know anything about this stuff, but maybe that's why it came to me and not them, because I was trying to understand how it all works instead of knowing it already.

"So, who was the vessel?" I ask. Surely, if the vessel is this important to keep things running smoothly, they would protect him or her.

"Nobody knows," the Alpha says, and Logan nods in agreement. "When someone is chosen, the goddess swears them to secrecy, for their own protection."

"Because if someone found out," Logan adds. "They might try to..."

His eyes go wide again as he trails off. He obviously just thought of something else, but this time, it's me who doesn't know where this is going.

Chapter Fourteen

~~Logan's PoV~~

I'm not quite sure how we've gone from talking about kissing to the conversation we're having now, but I'm really impressed with Sadie. She saw something so clearly that the rest of us had completely missed.

Of course the mating bond was messed up because something happened to the moon goddess' vessel. It's so obvious now that she said it, but it hadn't occurred to me nor to my dad or any of the other Alphas.

The vessels are one of the most shadowy and least understood parts of our werewolf culture. As my dad said, no one knows who they are, but we all know the legends, that the moon goddess would choose at least one person from an area to hold her power, to ensure that her plans were carried out. She visited them in person to make the transfer, so they were the only people who ever got to look on the goddess' face.

As far as I know, it's always a woman, and some people think the power is passed down by birth to her daughters, generation after generation, until a line dies out and the goddess chooses a new vessel.

That way, all the wolves in the world continue to receive her protection, even when she can't be with us.

I don't know what the goddess does with the rest of her time, but it's one of those things we were just never meant to know, I suppose.

And the issue with the mates is affecting us and the surrounding packs, but not all werewolves around the world. My dad has reached out to other packs further away and they aren't having any problems. So it makes sense that something has happened to *our* vessel, and no one else's.

This was all Sadie's idea, but what just occurred to me is: what if someone *wanted* this to happen? What if they did it on purpose? If they found out who the vessel was, they might have killed them intentionally to mess things up, to get us all confused and thrown off, though what they might want to accomplish by it, I'm sure.

And of course, when I think of anyone being hunted down on purpose, my thoughts go immediately to my mom and Kara.

Was my mom the vessel? Is that why they targeted her? And then they killed Kara too, because she would have inherited it? Since I was just a boy, they didn't have to worry about that, so they left me alive.

It makes sense. More sense than any other explanation I've ever come up with, and I share the idea with my dad to see if he agrees.

He listens to me carefully and there's a long silence when I finish. Sadie seems to be holding her breath waiting for him to respond, and I am too.

"I can see why you think that," he finally agrees. "But the mate bond wasn't affected when they died. That was a year ago, and the mix-ups only started happening recently."

My spirits instantly deflate. Damn it. I really thought I was onto something there. "So, who's died recently?" I ask, trying to hide the disappointment in my voice. "It wouldn't have to be in our pack, it could be any of the packs that are affected. It must be someone who was killed unnaturally. If we can find out who the vessel was and who killed them, maybe we can figure out what they're after."

My dad agrees and says he'll get in touch with all the other Alphas right away. He praises both Sadie and I for our contributions before hanging up.

"That was really smart," I tell her once we're on our own again.

Her cheeks flush as she looks down at her hands. "Not really. I think you just needed an outsider's perspective."

Maybe that's true. Sadie has a really different way of looking at things, and that brings me back to the whole reason we started this conversation in the first place.

When she told me that she likes me, I felt a happiness and hopefulness that I had never expected to feel again. It makes me feel glad and guilty all at the same time. Glad, obviously, because I like her too and I think we could be really good together. But guilty because I still need to wait for my mate, and also because this is just one more experience Kara never gets to have. It feels like I've taken over the life she was meant to have, and I wish it wasn't that way. I would gladly give it back to her.

Sadie's obviously not thinking about that right now though. She's still focused on the vessel. "So, if this vessel woman, whoever she was, was killed, why doesn't the moon goddess pick a new one?"

I have no answer for that. "I'm not sure. Maybe she doesn't know it happened?"

Sadie frowns. "I thought a goddess would know everything?"

I can only shrug. "I don't know. It's one more thing we need to figure out."

"There are quite a few of those things, aren't there?"

Is she talking about me and her now? Are we one of the things we need to figure out? I'm not sure, but I smile over at her. "We'll get there. I promise."

I don't know if that's a promise I can keep, but I do know that I'm going to do my very best.

~~Ava's PoV~~

I'm staring at the front door, waiting for Sadie to come home, so full of questions I think I might burst.

Finally, the door opens and I pounce on her before she even gets it closed behind her. "Is it true?!"

Sadie jumps from my sudden appearance. "God, Ava! You scared me!"

"Sorry," I apologize, though I'm not really. I just want her to answer the question. "I heard you and Logan and Micah went out today and Micah didn't come back. Is it true? Did he go rogue?"

It's been all anyone in the pack has been talking about for the last couple of hours. The Alpha felt someone sever themselves from the pack, but he didn't know right away who it was. Beta Aldric had to reach out to each of us by mind-link to confirm we were still here, and it was only when he got to his son, literally the last person on his list, that Micah failed to answer.

That led to a pack-wide search for Micah, and finally, the border guard said he saw Micah go with Logan and Sadie earlier today. Just ten minutes ago, news spread that Logan and Sadie were back but Micah wasn't with them.

Gossip spreads fast when you can all communicate telepathically, and I have the inside scoop since my cousin was one of the last people who had seen him.

A frown creases Sadie's face. "I guess so. He ditched us when we were in the city. Logan and I tried to find him, but we couldn't, so we had to come back. The Alpha called Logan in the car to ask what happened and that's when we found out he broke from the pack."

My eyes narrow as she speaks. There's something weird about the way she's saying all this, but I don't know what it is, or why she would lie.

"Did something else happen?" I ask, trying to guess what it might be.

Sadie glances around to make sure no one else can hear us.

"Mom and Dad are out," I assure her. "And Aaron's over at Laurel's."

He's been over there a lot lately. My wolf has gone quiet about her, so I suspect something has happened between them, but I don't know what it is. It's all still very confusing.

Now that she knows we're alone, Sadie walks to the living room and sits down on the couch. I sit across from her, waiting to hear what else she has to say.

"Micah kissed me last night."

My mouth falls open in shock. If I had a million guesses about what she had to tell me, it would never have been that. "Are you serious? Why?"

Sadie laughs. "Gee, thanks, Ava."

Oh, shit, I didn't mean it like that. "No, that's not what I... I just meant, I thought you guys hate each other!"

"We did," she admits with a shrug. "I guess he changed his mind."

"And what about you?" I ask, still confused. "I kind of thought you liked Logan."

It's not just me. Everyone in our class has noticed the way Logan has changed and how much time the two of them spend together.

"I do," she confesses, and my eyes go even wider, making her laugh again. "It's allowed, isn't it?"

"Of course," I tell her. "It's just, you've got the two hottest guys in school fighting over you? That's amazing! And completely unfair."

Sadie rolls her eyes. "They're hardly fighting over me. Logan just wants to be friends and Micah just left the pack."

"Did Logan actually say that?"

I'm surprised. I would have bet anything that he liked her too.

She nods. "He says he wants to wait and see who his mate is."

Ah, that makes sense, at least to me, but I can see Sadie doesn't agree. "Well, let's pretend they aren't both being idiots. Which of them would you choose?"

Sadie groans. "Come on, Ava."

"Seriously! Say Micah comes back tomorrow and Logan changes his mind, and they both show up here declaring their undying love. Which of them would you go for?"

"You watch way too many romance movies," she says, trying to stand up, but I'm not letting her get away that easily.

"It's a simple question," I tell her. "I know which one I'd go for."

That makes her curious. "Really? Who would you pick?"

Before I can answer, the front door opens and Aaron and Laurel come in, holding hands. They're both looking a lot happier.

"Hey, guys," my brother greets us. "Are Mom and Dad here?"

I shake my head. "No, they're not back yet. Why?"

Aaron looks at Laurel and they share a small smile. "We've got something to tell them," he says to me.

More gossip? This day is getting better and better. "What is it?"

"Maybe we should wait for your parents," Sadie suggests.

"No, it's okay," Aaron tells her. "Everyone's going to know soon enough."

He pulls down the collar of his shirt to show off Laurel's mark, and I gasp. Loudly.

"Oh my goddess! You didn't!" I'm shocked. My brother and his straight-arrow girlfriend really marked each other without being mates? That must be why my wolf has been so quiet.

"What is that?" Sadie asks, looking concerned. "Did something bite you?"

The rest of us laugh. "It was me," Laurel admits, pulling down her own shirt to show us her matching mark. "And Aaron bit me too."

"They marked each other," I explain to Sadie. "They've chosen each other as mates."

A new light fires in Sadie's eyes. "So, you *can* choose?"

"It's not encouraged," I tell her honestly. "But yeah, if you really want to, you can."

CLAIMING MY WOLF

"I don't know if we technically need to reject each other?" Laurel asks me, and I can only shrug. I have no idea either. That's a question for the Alpha, I guess, but for now, I jump up and hug my brother and his mate.

"I'm really happy for you both."

"Me too," Sadie agrees with a genuine smile.

"Thanks, guys." Aaron looks touched by our support. "Let's just hope the rest of the pack takes it as well as you two."

He sounds a bit nervous and I don't blame him. Wolves used to get punished for going against their fated mate bond, but surely, everyone will see this is a special circumstance.

This was the way it was meant to be, I'm sure of it. I only hope that there's a second chance mate out there waiting for me.

~~Logan's PoV~~

The next morning, I meet my dad in the pack house kitchen before dawn.

"Have a big breakfast," he warns me. "We might be gone for a while and I don't know how much food they'll have."

We're going to a neighboring pack for a big meeting with all the Alphas of the other packs who have been affected by the mating problems. Each Alpha has been asked to bring a list of any pack members who died in the week or two prior to when the problem with the mates began. We'll be reviewing all of them to try to identify who the vessel was and who might have wanted that person dead.

It still isn't clear how that's going to help us fix the problem, but at least it's a place to start.

My dad goes over a few last things with Beta Aldric, who will be in charge of the pack while we're away, and we both head out to the car.

My dad's security team is following us in another vehicle, but in the car, it's just the two of us. It's been a while since we were alone in a confined space like this for so long.

"We haven't really talked about your birthday," my dad says as we get out onto the highway. "With everything else going on, it's kind of slipped through the cracks."

I haven't really given it much thought either. It's only a few days away and usually, there would be a pack-wide celebration for the next Alpha, to celebrate him gaining his wolf, and also to see if he finds his mate. Since we're unable to put any faith in the mate bond right now, the second part seems kind of pointless.

People will still want to see my wolf though. It's important for the pack, so it's important to me.

"We should do it," I tell him. Normally, the Luna would organize this kind of thing though, and I don't have a clue where to start. "Who's going to plan it?"

My dad laughs. "I thought maybe you and your friends could. You've been spending a lot of time with Sadie lately."

He's obviously fishing for information, so I refuse to answer. "That's none of your business."

He grins. "Which means there's some business going on?"

I roll my eyes at this sudden interest in my personal life. "I'm not talking about this with you."

"Why not?" he asks. "I'm sure I'm a much better source than a bunch of high school boys on how to woo a woman."

"Woo? Seriously?" What century are we in?

"Court?" he suggests instead, his eyes twinkling with amusement. He's obviously enjoying this.

"You're 40, Dad, not 100," I say, which makes him laugh. "And Sadie and I are just friends."

"You can't tell me I'm not old and then pretend I'm blind, Logan." Once again, I roll my eyes, and he laughs again. "Fine, you don't have to tell me, but just know I'm here if you have any questions."

"Questions?"

I don't know what he's talking about.

"Technical questions," he clarifies. "How to do certain things."

I can't believe we're talking about this. "I have the internet, Dad. I'll be fine."

"Don't believe everything you see online," he warns, still chuckling.

Thankfully, he changes the subject and we talk about far less personal things for the rest of the trip, but I can't stop the smile that pulls at my lips when it crosses my mind again. We haven't had many regular father and son moments in the last year. It's kind of nice, even when he is being totally embarrassing.

Most of the other Alphas are already there when we arrive, so my dad introduces me to everyone. I've met many of them before, but this is the first time I'm taking part in something like this in an official capacity. It's clear to me how much respect everyone has for my dad, and I want more than ever to make him and my pack proud.

When everyone arrives, we sit down around the large oval table and start going through the lists that everyone brought with them. There aren't that many deaths in the period we're looking at, and most of them are obviously natural causes. There's one accident in the Wild Prairie pack, but the Alpha lays out all the facts and it sounds like it was genuinely an accident. If someone planned it, they covered their tracks well.

It seems we're at a dead end, until I remember one *other* accident that took place: the one that brought Sadie to our pack in the first place.

"Dad," I whisper to get his attention. "What about Mrs Jennings?"

Realization dawns in his eyes. She isn't on our list because she technically wasn't a pack member at the time. But she *used* to be part of our pack, she was still a wolf who lived in the area, and her death coincides almost perfectly with the beginning of our troubles.

I already thought the 'accident' sounded a little suspicious and now, there's even more reason to think so.

And if Sadie's mom was the vessel, and the powers got passed down to the vessel's daughter...

I cover my hand to keep my gasp in. *Holy fuck*. Sadie is the next vessel.

She just must not know it yet. Maybe it won't take hold until she gets her wolf. Will the moon goddess actually appear to her?

The idea of skeptical Sadie coming face-to-face with the goddess almost makes me smile, until I realize one more thing.

If she's the next vessel, that must be why someone wants her dead.

Chapter Fifteen

~~**Micah's PoV**~~

It's my fourth night hanging out at the rogue bar in the city. I found myself a cheap bed at a hostel where I can spend my nights, I spend the days just wandering the city, and in the evening, I come to the bar.

The first night, I got into a fight. It wasn't my fault, or at least not entirely. Nobody would give me the time of day when I first arrived and I was scanning the room, trying to figure out who would be most likely to talk to me. Apparently, I looked at someone the wrong way, and instead of apologizing when he confronted me, I told him to fuck off. We brawled right there in the bar and I more than held my own. I would have won if the bartender hadn't come to tear us apart before we shifted, and people knew it too. After that, they were all a bit more friendly.

Well, they stopped ignoring me, at least.

A few people talked and drank with me over the next couple of nights. I dropped some hints just like Logan, Sadie and I had planned out. I told people I'd just left my pack after a dispute with my asshole father. I made sure I said the name of the pack. And I let it be known I was desperate for cash and willing to do some dirty work to earn it.

But so far, no one has been biting.

I spoke to Logan last night and he filled me in on what's been happening at the pack since I left. Everyone was shocked at my defection. He said my dad refused to even talk about it with the Alpha, telling him that he was fine when the Alpha asked. I'm not even surprised. Maybe he *is* fine. Maybe he doesn't care.

Then Logan tells me all about Sadie's theory about the vessel being killed, and how they'd determined that Sadie's mom must have been the vessel, and that Sadie herself would most likely take on the role once she gained her wolf. They figure this is why the person after her is targeting her in the first place.

The idea terrifies me and I demand to know what they're doing to keep Sadie safe. If someone already killed her parents over this, they're not messing around. He promises me that she's being watched 24 hours a day. It upsets me that I'm not there to keep an eye on her myself until Logan reminds me that it's more important than ever now that we find out who's behind the attacks.

Sadie's life is in my hands now.

I ask Logan why the person behind all this hasn't made a move yet. If they were wanting to break the mate bond and it happened, why not do whatever they wanted to do now, before Sadie gets her wolf? Why worry about killing her first?

"My dad has a theory about that," he explains. "He thinks because the next vessel is still alive but without her wolf, the mate bond is only partially affected. New bonds aren't forming properly, but the existing bonds are fine."

I think I understand. "So if Sadie dies, then ALL mate bonds will be broken?" That would be chaos.

"We think so," Logan confirms. "We think that's what the person behind this is after. But we'd rather not find out."

No kidding. If someone wanted to take over the whole territory, it was about the best way to ensure the packs weren't able to defend themselves. Everyone who lost their mate would be weakened and broken-hearted.

I promise to do everything I can, but so far, it's been limited to sitting in this bar, nursing a beer and trying to look desperate. I feel fucking useless.

"Are you the wolf from Westbridge?"

The voice startles me out of my thoughts. A woman stands in front of me, probably in her 30s or 40s. I've seen her in here a few times but she's never paid any attention to me before. She looks hard and she stinks of rogue, though so does everyone in here.

So do I, for that matter.

"That's me," I reply as nonchalantly as I can. "Who wants to know?"

"My boss."

My heart beats faster as I keep my expression neutral. This might be what I've been waiting for. "Who's your boss?"

"That's above your paygrade, kid," she sneers. "But if you want money, I suggest you come with me."

I've got nothing better to do, so I drain the rest of my beer and slam the empty bottle down on the table. "Let's go."

She leads me through a door into the back storeroom of the bar, and through another door into a small windowless room where a man sits at a table, two larger men standing behind him. I've never seen any of them before.

The whole scene reminds me of a mafia movie, where nothing good ever happens to the guy in my shoes, but I do my best to look unafraid as the woman gestures to the other chair on the opposite side of the table.

I sit down as casually as I can. "You've got a job for me?"

"If you can handle it," the guy replies. "I need someone who can get into Westbridge."

My heart kicks into an even higher gear. This definitely sounds like the guy I've been looking for.

"Lived there my whole life," I reply. "Until the old man got on my last nerve."

I hope I sound tough and not like someone just pretending to be. The man's expression doesn't change.

"You went to school there?" he asks.

I nod. "Until last week, yeah."

"So, you know the students? Do you know a new student who just moved there?"

This is definitely our guy. Fuck yes, I've found him. I have to fight not to show my satisfaction.

"We don't get many new students," I tell him honestly. "So, I'm guessing you're talking about Sadie Jennings."

The man's eyes glint in the dim lighting. He's pleased with that answer, just as pleased as I was with his.

"Precisely. Do you know where to find her?"

I nod. "Yeah, I know which house she's in, which classes she's in, all of it. Why?"

I already know the answer, of course, but I need to hear him say it.

"We need her taken out," he responds, like it's a perfectly reasonable thing to say. "My employer will pay very well if you're successful."

His employer? Fuck. He's just a middle man. I need the top guy.

"I need to know who I'm working for," I try, crossing my arms defiantly. "I'll take the job, but only if I can meet him first."

"That's not possible," the man says. "He's very busy."

He. That was something, at least, but not enough to go on.

"Then I guess we're done here," I tell him, getting to my feet. "Good luck finding someone else who knows the pack as well as I do."

He says nothing as I walk to the door and for a moment, I'm afraid he's going to call my bluff. But just as I reach for the handle, he calls out to me.

"Fine. You can meet him tomorrow, same time, back here. But once you do, there's no going back. If you meet with him, you do the job, or you die."

I can work with that. "I'll see you tomorrow then."

~~Sadie's PoV~~

It's been weird without Micah at school this week. I didn't realize just how much I associated him with the place, for better or for worse. I keep expecting to see his face as I round every corner or glance over at his empty desk.

I miss him, I have to admit, but is it as a friend, or something more? That, I'm not so sure about. I keep thinking about the way he kissed me. I wish we had a chance to talk about it, but that won't be possible until he comes back.

Meanwhile, Logan is still being friendly but not too friendly. I've been hanging out with Ally and Emma more since I have more free time, even though I'm still being watched constantly by my protection detail.

Logan called me on Sunday when he got back from the Alpha meeting with his dad to tell me about how they think my mom was the vessel and that I'm supposed to be the next one. They figure someone caused my parents' accident on purpose and that the same person is the one behind the attempted attacks on me.

I have to admit it makes sense, but that would also mean admitting that there really is a moon goddess and that my mother met her, and I'm still having a hard time with that. I agree to the extra security because I don't really have much choice, and I keep my doubts about the rest of it to myself.

I think Logan knows I don't really believe it, and it feels like it's putting more distance between us, which isn't what I want at all.

But I can't just pretend to believe in something I don't either, so I don't know what else to do.

"Hi, everyone," Logan's deep voice says as I sit outside talking with Ally and Emma. Spring is definitely here now, the days are a lot warmer and all the snow is gone. I had my back to the school so I didn't see him walking over to us.

"Hey, Logan," they both reply and I say hello too, without turning around.

"Can I borrow Sadie for a minute?" he asks my friends, and they both give me excited smiles before excusing themselves and I have to try hard not to roll my eyes. Whatever he wants to talk to me about, I know it's not what they think it is.

"What's up?" I ask, turning to face him. It's the first time I've seen him today and he looks good. My stomach does a little flip at his closeness, even though I tell myself I'm being stupid to get my hopes up. Every time I hope, I just get disappointed.

"I talked to Micah again last night," he says, keeping his voice low as he sits down across from me. "He's made some progress."

Instantly, I'm on the edge of my seat, my own problems forgotten. "What happened?"

He tells me everything Micah told him about the meeting and how he's supposed to be meeting with the real boss tonight.

"That's great," I say sincerely when he finishes. "He's doing really well."

"He is," Logan agrees. "Hopefully, we'll get some answers soon and we can put a stop to the whole thing."

That would be nice. One less thing to worry about, anyway.

"Are you... uh, planning to come to the party tomorrow?" he asks, suddenly looking a bit nervous.

The party. He means his birthday party. It's the first time he's mentioned it to me even though it's all anybody at school's been talking about all week. The whole pack is invited, so I know I don't need a personal invitation from him, but it would have been nice to get one anyway.

"I'm not sure I want to see what kind of party Blair and Tonya are throwing," I tell him honestly, which makes him laugh.

Ava told me Logan asked them to plan the party partly because they've thrown a lot of parties before, and partly to give Blair a distraction. She seems pretty upset about Micah leaving. They must have been closer than I realized, which only makes his declaration about liking me before he left even more strange.

"But it's your birthday," I continue. "Of course I'll be there."

His genuinely pleased smile makes my stomach flutter again. "I'm glad. I'll see you there, then."

He walks away and I watch him go, my mind racing. What happens if Logan finds his mate tomorrow and it's not me? He wouldn't act on it, since there's still the Alpha's hold on all new bonds, but it would have to make him wonder.

Or even worse, what if somehow, it *is* me, but he thinks it's not true because all the bonds are going wrong?

I don't see a good way this can go, but I know I don't really have a choice. I'm going to have to go and find out for myself.

~~**Logan's PoV**~~

I wait by my phone all night for Micah's call, but when it comes, it's not the news either of us wanted.

"The guy didn't show," he growls into the phone. "I wasted the whole night waiting until they finally told me he'd been held up by something and couldn't get away. They promise he'll show up tomorrow instead."

That's frustrating, but there really isn't anything we can do about it other than wait and try again tomorrow. "Thanks, Micah. I might not be able to get to my phone right away tomorrow because of the party, but leave a message when you know anything."

"Right. Happy birthday, man," he tells me. "Sorry I'm going to miss it."

"Yeah, me too." It'll be weird not having Micah there, we've been at each other's parties our whole lives.

After we hang up, I go down to talk to my dad, just to see if there's any news, but he's in an emergency meeting with Beta Aldric and the defense team. They figure someone might try to attack tomorrow during the party while we're all distracted, so my dad wants extra security. There's not much I can contribute to that discussion, so I leave them alone and go back to my room.

For about the hundredth time this week, I pick up my phone to call Sadie and put it down again. Things are weird between us right now, and I don't know how to fix it. I miss talking to her. It's actually kind of crazy how much I miss it, considering we really haven't known each other that long.

The next day is a rush of activity. I still have to go to school, but it feels like every single person in the whole pack wants to come up and wish me a happy birthday. I know they all mean it sincerely so I'm as gracious as I can be about the whole thing. When school ends, I'm relieved to go home, but the pack house is even worse, full of people setting up for the party and wanting a bit of my time. By the time I get to my room to change for the night, I'm already exhausted.

I put on my best shirt, a deep green color that my mom used to say looked good with my eyes, and a pair of black dress pants. After spending a little bit of time on my hair, I head back downstairs. I'm impressed with what Blair and Tonya have put together, and when they spot me and come to see what I think, I tell them honestly that it's amazing.

They've set up big tents in the backyard of the pack house with lights strung all around. There are tables full of food and a big dance floor with a DJ and even a photo booth, for some reason. If it had been left up to me, it would have been a plate of hamburgers and Spotify hooked up to some speakers. I'm glad I asked them to look after it.

People start arriving and they all want to talk to me too. I try to keep an eye out for Sadie, but it's impossible, there are just too many people. The Millers all come over to congratulate me but Sadie's not with them.

"Did Sadie come?" I ask Ava quietly before they step away. She said she would, but maybe she changed her mind.

"She's here," Ava tells me. "I think she just went to get some food."

That reminds me that I'm hungry too, so I manage to break away and head for the food table and that's where I see her.

She's wearing a mid-length silver dress that shines under the lights, her dark hair done up in a big braided pattern. I have no idea what it's called, but it looks nice. I want to tell her so, but I hold myself back.

"Hey," I greet her casually, trying to pretend I haven't been looking for her all night.

"Hey, yourself." She gives me a warm smile. "You're certainly Mr Popular tonight."

I shrug. "One night a year, I guess."

She laughs. "I don't know about that. They all really love you. The whole pack, I mean."

They do. It's one of the best things about being in a pack, and I hope she can see that. "I care about them all too. More than anything."

Her smile falters just a bit. "Yeah, I get that. Well, happy birthday, Logan."

Shit. I just realized that it sounded like I care about them more than her, and I try to stop her from walking away, but someone else grabs my shoulder, wanting to say happy birthday, and I have no choice but to turn and smile politely even though I'm kicking myself internally.

Finally, it's time for my wolf to appear and as I stand up in front of the crowd, feeling all their energy and attention focused on me, for the first time, I really stop and appreciate this day for what it is. This is the day I've been waiting my whole life for, the day I'll finally be a fully-fledged werewolf.

The sun dips below the horizon and I feel a strange tightening feeling in my head. A few seconds later, I hear him.

Logan. The voice in my head is deep, even deeper than my own, and full of authority. *I'm here.*

What's your name?

Shadow. The goddess has great plans for you, for us both.

Really? I wasn't expecting him to say anything like that, but I'm excited to hear it. Who wouldn't be? First, though, I want to give him a warning. *There's something wrong with the mate bonds right now. Even if you think you see our mate, it's probably not true.*

He's silent for a moment as my eyes scan the crowd, letting him take a look. Finally, he answers me. *I don't see her.*

That's a relief, I guess. At least I don't have to deal with disappointing anyone.

I strip down to my underwear and complete my first shift for the pack, which is what everyone's here to see. There's a great cheer among everyone as I take my wolf form, and I let Shadow take control, running through the woods to the lake where I can see myself reflected. My wolf is big and midnight black, and I feel almost complete.

But only *almost*, because there's still something missing.

Suddenly, I know exactly what it is.

When I get back to the party, some people are dancing and others, mostly those with little kids, are leaving. I shift back and get dressed again before going to find Sadie. She's with her friends, and once again, I intrude to ask to speak to her alone.

We go into the pack house library and she gives me a teasing smile. "If you keep doing that, people are going to think there's something going on between us."

"Maybe they *should* think that," I hear myself saying.

Sadie's eyes widen, her smile vanishing into uncertainty. "What do you mean?"

"I mean, I've been an idiot, Sadie, and I'm sorry. You were right."

"About what?" She's still not sure what I'm trying to say, which is totally my fault. I guess I'm not saying it very well.

"I want there to be something going on between us. I like you, Sadie, and I'm tired of pretending I don't."

With those words, I kiss her, and somehow, it's even better than it was the first time. I can feel Shadow's contentment in my head. Maybe that means she's my mate and maybe it doesn't, but for the first time, I don't really care.

Chapter Sixteen

~~**Micah's PoV**~~

It's Friday night and while the rest of my pack is celebrating the next Alpha's birthday, I'm stuck in this dirty bar again. I wonder what Sadie's wearing tonight. She looked amazing at Ava and Aaron's party, and the memory makes me smile.

"You look like you're thinking of something good," a woman's voice says and I blink to find her standing right in front of me. "Want to make it a reality?"

I've seen her a few times over the last week, enough times to know what she's offering. Every so often, she leaves the room with a different male wolf and comes back ten minutes later with enough cash for another drink. Young, old, doesn't seem to matter.

"Piss off," I growl at her. "I'm waiting for someone."

She shrugs, not offended by my rudeness, and wanders off to try her luck elsewhere.

"Mr Geary?" someone else says a minute later. This time, it's the same wolf from the other night, the one who took me to the meeting in the first place. "They're ready for you."

Finally. It was fun to do this for the first few days, but I'm getting tired of it now. I'm ready for some action, and more than anything, ready to get back to my pack. I didn't know quite how much I liked being a part of it until I wasn't.

She takes me back to the same room from the night before, and the same guy is waiting for me with the same two goons behind him. I look around, hoping I'm missing something, but there's no one else there and I start to get frustrated. "What is this? I told you I wanted to talk to your boss."

"You will," the man says, gesturing to the seat across from him. "Take a seat."

Since I don't have much choice, I sit down.

"I've just been asked to double check that you still want to do this," he tells me. "This is your last chance to back out. Otherwise..."

"I do the job or you kill me," I say, filling in the rest of the sentence. "I've got it. Let's move this along."

He raises his eyebrows at me, but turns to one of the men behind him and gives him a nod. That guy leaves the room, closing the door behind him.

"Once you've met with my employer, you'll be leaving tonight to carry out the task," the guy sitting down tells me. "There won't be time for you to go home again."

That's a bit of a problem. I won't have a way of getting any information to Logan then, but I shrug like it's no big deal. "Fine. It's not like I have much of a home right now anyway."

The ghost of a smile crosses his face. "Indeed. But if you're successful, you might find yourself a new home with us."

"Us?" I repeat.

"The new pack that is going to run the whole territory," he explains. "Under our new Alpha."

He looks to the door which opens at just that moment. I turn to see who he's talking about, and my jaw drops open when I see who walks in.

"Dad?"

This can't be real. I blink quickly, as if I might be seeing things, but it's him alright. His scent gives him away even if I couldn't see him for myself.

"Leave us, all of you," he orders and everyone else immediately leaves the room. He sits down across from me as I try to make some sense of what the fuck is going on.

I hope that somehow he found out what I was doing and decided to teach me a lesson. I hope that this is all a setup, that it's anything other than what it seems like.

Which is that my dad is a fucking traitor.

"You really couldn't leave well enough alone, could you?" he says as he leans back in his chair, looking me over coldly. "Had to try and play the hero?"

"This is why you shot down my idea about sending someone undercover?" I ask, trying to put all the pieces together in my head. "Because it would lead back to you?"

"I've covered my tracks very carefully," he says, like it's something to be proud of. "You weren't supposed to get involved. It would have been better if you didn't know. But now you're here, and the truth is, I need you. With all the extra protection they've put on her, you're the only one that can get close to her."

My heart sinks even further as I realize what he's saying. "You actually think I'm going to kill Sadie?"

"That's what you agreed to, isn't it?" He smirks at me. "You said you'd do the job, or you die."

"You know I'm just here to expose them," I growl back at him. "To expose *you*, you son of a..."

"I know that was your plan," he cuts me off. "But things have changed, haven't they? Now, you've got a choice, Micah. You can do as I say, or you'll die. Who's going to notice one missing rogue? You're cut off from the pack. You're all on your own."

"I'm your son," I can't help pointing out, my face screwing up in disbelief. What the fuck is wrong with him?

"And if you join me, if you make me proud, there might be a place for you in the new order," he says.

Make him proud? When have I ever done that? I tried so hard for so long, and it turns out he was never someone I should have been trying to impress in the first place.

"What is all this about?" I ask. I still don't see the big picture. "What do you want?"

He leans forward, his gaze hot and intense. "I want wolves to be what we used to be. I want to stop this mating with humans and diluting our bloodlines. I want us to be strong and unbeatable, and if I have to break a few things to make things better, then I'm prepared to do it."

Break a few things? "You killed Sadie's parents."

My eyes widen in horror as I realize it must be true.

He doesn't even try to deny it. "I would have done it sooner, but It took me a long time to figure out who the second vessel was."

What is he talking about? "The second one?" I repeat. "Who was the first?"

He huffs in disbelief. "You really haven't figured it out yet? Pathetic."

I start to growl at the insult but a second later, it hits me. "The Luna. She was a vessel too."

Of course. She was attacked on purpose and killed, and Kara along with her, because it would have passed to her.

"They were together the night the moon goddess came, the Luna and Sadie's mother," he tells me. "She passed her gift to them both. I've gotten rid of the two vessels and one of the heirs. There's just one left, and you're going to finish it."

"And then what?" I ask, trying to work out the last part of the plan. "After Sadie dies, what will you do?"

"I have an army ready to go. As soon as the mate bonds break, we'll strike before they can muster any defense. We'll take over the whole area and set up a new kingdom, a place where wolves can be wolves again."

"With you as the king," I guess.

"Of course."

He's mad. He's completely insane. At last, I see it clearly.

However, I have no choice. He won't hesitate to kill me if I refuse, so I try my best to look like the whole thing excites me.

"If you're the king, does that make me a prince?"

~~Sadie's PoV~~

I'm so tired of Logan being hot and cold with me. When he came over to the food table earlier, it almost felt like he was looking for me, and the look that he gave me when he saw me in my dress suggested he liked what he found. But then he talked again about how important the pack was to him and I got the message, loud and clear. The pack was more important than me and it always would be. His obligations outweighed anything he might be feeling.

So, I told myself I didn't care. If he wanted to just be friends, then we'd just be friends. But when he got up in front of the crowd to do his first shift, stripping down to his underwear in front of everyone, my body flushed with heat. It was obvious from the very first time we met just how big and strong he was, but seeing him wearing almost nothing was almost too much to take.

Just friends, my ass.

At least he didn't seem to recognize anyone as his mate, so that was one less worry, but as I watched him change into a large black wolf, it reminded me again just how crazy this whole thing was.

My birthday is coming up soon too. Is that really going to happen to me?

I almost left right after Logan's wolf ran off into the woods, but Ally and Emma stopped me, and I was still talking to them when Logan came back. He asked to talk to me, took me inside the house to the library, and he kissed me.

And now, I *really* don't know what to think.

It's just as good as our kiss in the kitchen a week ago, or maybe even better. I can feel his certainty this time. All the hesitation that was there before is gone and now, it's just me and him and this special electricity that seems to exist between us.

"Can you forgive me for being an idiot?" he asks, separating his lips from mine just long enough to ask the question. Before I can even answer, he's kissing me again like he can't get enough of it.

I can't either.

His body is warm, probably because he's just been running, and now that I know what it looks like beneath his clothes, I want to feel it for myself too. My hands run across his hard chest and I feel it rumble beneath my fingers with something that almost sounds like a growl.

Logan's hands thread through my hair, pulling me tighter to him, and as our bodies press against each other, I feel him starting to grow harder. Technically, he's an adult today, and that's more than evident in the size of him.

A noise just outside the door makes us both jump apart. We hear a laugh and two voices talking as they walk by, moving further down the hall.

"This isn't very private," Logan complains.

I have to laugh. "You're surprised that your massive, over-the-top birthday party has people at it?"

He narrows his eyes at me, but I can see he's trying not to smile. "The party wasn't my choice. I had to do it."

"Because you're the chosen one, I get it," I tease him, and his green eyes darken. He likes that I don't take him too seriously, I can tell.

"I think I've made enough of an appearance," he says, taking a step closer so our faces are almost touching again. "Do you want to come upstairs with me?"

Upstairs? To his room? I wasn't expecting that and a shot of both nervousness and anticipation runs through me.

I'm not sure exactly what he has in mind, but I'm willing to find out. "I'd like that."

With a smile, he takes my hand before going to the door and opening it just a crack. With a quick glance in both directions, he checks the coast is clear and pulls me along towards the big staircase in the center of the house, both of us grinning like kids who've just stolen the last cookie from the cookie jar.

It's two flights of stairs up to the floor with his room, and we run the whole way, laughing and panting by the time we reach the top. Logan pulls me towards him again, kissing me as he pushes me back against the wall in the hallway.

His kiss is stronger and more urgent, and I'm sure mine is too. I've never wanted anything like I want him right now.

Finally, he seems to realize we haven't actually got to his room yet, and he lets me go, but only enough to lead me down the hall and through an open door.

It's dark in the room, but not totally black. The full moon shines through the window, letting us see our way as Logan closes the door behind us, leaving the lights off. We stumble together, our lips connected again, until we hit the edge of his bed, and the next thing I know we're falling together onto it, his arms wrapped around me as I land on top of him.

He's even harder now, the length of his cock making me gasp in surprise as my weight settles on top of it.

"I don't want to rush you," he tells me even as the evidence of his arousal presses against me. "We can take things as slow or fast as you want."

"Have you done this with a lot of girls?" I can't help asking. I won't judge him for it, I just want to know how our levels of experience compare.

However, he shakes his head. "I've never even had a girl in here before, Sadie. I've never done anything more than kiss. I hope that's okay."

Okay? My heart melts at the idea of this strong, handsome man being worried about disappointing me. "I haven't really done much either," I admit. "I was waiting for something special."

I can just make out his uncertain eyes in the moonlight. "Is this special for you?"

Does he really have to ask?

"It's the most special," I tell him, leaning down to kiss him again.

~~Micah's PoV~~

On the road back to Westbridge, my dad fills me in with his plan for how this is all going to go down.

"We can't take you in as a rogue," he explains. "It would alert the border guards right away."

"I'm not going in?" Then what am I doing here?

He sighs, looking unimpressed. "Of course you're going in, but we have to bring you back into the pack first."

"Oh." I'm still confused, though I don't want to admit it. I thought only the Alpha could restore my standing to the pack.

My dad sees my confusion even though I'm trying to hide it, and he rolls his eyes. "I already had the Alpha grant me temporary authority to return you to the pack myself if I found you. Of course he understood, as one father to another."

Of course he did. That was what a *normal* father would want. How could my dad sit there and compare himself to the Alpha when it came to being a father? They couldn't be more different. And he probably gave the Alpha some sob story about how sorry he was about me leaving, when all he was doing was plotting how to use me to get what he wanted.

This is actually great news, though. If my pack link is restored, it means I can mind-link and let people know what's going on. In particular, I can let Logan know. He'll have his wolf by now too, since the sun just went down, and he'll be able to link for the first time. It's kind of awesome that his first link will be one this important.

It'll be a good story for us to be able to share when we're Alpha and Beta.

"Then what?" I ask, trying to keep my dad talking. "You bring me back into the pack and we go in, and what happens next?"

"Logan's party will still be going on," he reminds me. "Some of my men will create a distraction, and you go to Sadie. Convince her you're there to protect her, and then, when you're close enough, pierce her skin with this."

He holds out a small dagger to me, sheathed in a leather scabbard. It's beautiful despite its purpose.

"I'm supposed to stab her?" I ask. That sounds pretty messy. I thought he wanted to avoid suspicion, and that would definitely lead to an investigation.

"Is that what I said?" my father snaps at me. "You don't need to stab her. The blade is poisoned, just get it into her bloodstream and it'll take care of the rest. You could almost do it in plain sight and no one would notice."

"How quickly after she dies will the mate bonds break?" I want to understand the whole plan so I have as much evidence as possible to take to the Alpha.

"Immediately," he predicts, his eyes gleaming at the idea. "My whole army is on standby, gathering outside all the packs in the area. By the morning, the world will be completely different, Micah. A new world. *Our* world."

Sounds more like Crazy Town to me, but whatever. This is all good news too. After I warn Logan and Sadie, I can tell the Alpha and he can contact all the other Alphas. They can find my dad's men waiting outside their territories, and hopefully, the whole operation can be brought down tonight.

"Now, give me your hand," he instructs. "It's time to come back home."

I hold my palm out to him and he pulls out another blade to make the cut. After slicing his own palm, he presses our hands together and murmurs a few words under his breath. Almost immediately, I feel my link to the pack returning. The emptiness in my head is gone, replaced by the reassuring presence of the rest of the pack instead.

"I'll hold onto this until we get to the party," my dad says, picking up the poisoned dagger as he lets go of my hand. "And if you even think about linking with anyone, it will be your throat that takes this blade. Understood?"

I swallow as his words sink in. He's going to be watching me. If my eyes glaze over, the sure-fire way to know a werewolf is mind-linking, he's going to slit my throat with his poisoned blade.

I wish I could say I thought he was bluffing, but I know he's not. I'm going to have to stay silent until I can get away from him.

I only hope that will give me enough time.

"This is happening tonight whether you're successful or not," he adds. "If you fail, I will do it myself. I would rather not, for both our sakes', but I will if I have to."

I understand that perfectly clearly too. If I fail, he's going to kill me. He's got it set up so either I die or Sadie does, or even both. I don't see yet how I'm going to avoid that.

The party's still going on when we get to the pack house, and my dad makes a big show of bringing me over to the Alpha and telling him I've repented. The Alpha looks genuinely happy to see me, but asks me to come and talk to him in the morning. I imagine I'm in for a lecture if nothing else, but that's the least of my worries right now.

"Where's Logan?" I ask, looking around at all the people dancing. I don't see him, or Sadie either.

"He went inside a few minutes ago," the Alpha says. "Hold on, let me find out. I know he'll want to see you."

His eyes cloud as he links with his son, and I try not to show my frustration. So much for my cool first link story. Nothing about this night is going well so far.

The Alpha frowns as his eyes clear. "He says he's gone up to his room, I guess all the excitement of the day tired him out."

I frown too. That doesn't really sound like Logan. He doesn't shirk his responsibilities to the pack.

"I'm sure he wouldn't mind if you go up and say hi though," he continues.

It sounds like he didn't mention to Logan that I'm here. I'd be happy to go up and talk to him now, that would be perfect actually, but my dad shakes his head at me. Obviously, he doesn't want me and Logan talking.

"I don't want to bother him," I say to appease my dad. "I'll see him tomorrow."

But to my surprise, the Alpha insists. "Nonsense, he'll want to see you. I'm heading upstairs myself. I'll walk up with you."

My dad intervenes. "Alpha, although I am pleased that Micah has returned, he will still be punished for his desertion. Not seeing his friends will be part of that punishment."

The Alpha, however, won't be put off. "We can give them a minute, Aldric. They've been best friends forever and it's Logan's birthday. Besides, I could use your help with something. Why don't you come up too and as soon as we're done, you can take Micah home?"

My dad has no good excuse not to go along with that, and I feel a lot more hopeful as we head up the stairs. At least if I can warn Logan, he can alert the others and make sure Sadie's safe. Then I'll just have to figure out how to stop my dad from killing me before he gets arrested.

We get to Logan's bedroom door and the Alpha gives me a nod. "Go on in. Aldric, come with me."

My dad gives me a warning look as he comes closer and, just out of view of the Alpha, presses the sheathed dagger into my hand. "Use it on him too if you have to," he whispers, like it's a perfectly normal thing to kill my best friend. I nod as meekly as I can to convince him he can count on me.

Which, of course, he can't.

As they walk away, I knock quickly on Logan's door and let myself in. It's dark inside, so I flip the light on, and that's when I see them.

Logan and Sadie, half-naked, tangled together on the bed.

Chapter Seventeen

~~Logan's PoV~~

I can't believe this is really happening.

Sadie's hands run down my bare chest in the darkness of my room. She just pulled my shirt off, taking the lead, and the feel of her fingers against my bare skin is electric as her mouth finds mine again. I've never felt this kind of desire, this kind of need, this kind of energy.

It just feels *right.*

I don't know if the tingles that her touch causes are a sign of a mate bond or if it's just something about her, but at this point, it hardly makes any difference.

For a moment, I think I hear voices outside my room, but her tongue collides with mine again and I forget everything but the feel of her, the smell of her, the taste of her. With a possessive growl, I reach behind her and pull down the zipper of her shiny, silver dress. It sparkles in the dim moonlight that's coming in my window.

Then, suddenly, the whole room goes bright and I wince as I look towards the door, trying to figure out what just happened.

My mouth drops open as I see Micah standing there, just inside the closed door, and he's looking at me just the same, looking at me and Sadie with his lips parted like he can't believe what he's seeing.

Sadie quickly gets off me, her hands going to her chest to stop her unzipped dress from falling down. "Micah?" she asks, the word coming out as a squeak and a guilty look on her face. "What are you doing here?"

That's a damn good question. Why is he in my room, and why is he in the pack at all? I sniff the air and am surprised that he doesn't have the rogue smell anymore.

What the fuck is going on?

He blinks twice, his jaw tight, before he seems to snap out of it. His eyes move to Sadie, a cold, hard expression on his face.

"I've come to kill you."

What? I jump to my feet, ready to protect her, before I even realize what I'm doing.

Micah huffs bitterly as he looks over at me. "Not really, of course. But that's what he thinks. That's why he brought me here."

I'm completely lost. "What who thinks?" Does that mean he found out who's behind all of this?

Micah looks back towards the door. "We don't have much time. They don't know Sadie's here, they think it's just you in here and I'm supposed to be wishing you a happy birthday."

His voice is still cold as he looks at me, and I don't feel like he's wishing me very much happiness right now at all. What is he so angry about? What happened since the last time we talked?

"Someone brought you here to kill Sadie?" I ask, trying to make sense of what he's saying. "You met the boss? You know who it is?"

"I know," he confirms, but he doesn't sound very happy about that either. "And he's got a backup plan, and probably a backup plan for his backup plan. If I don't do it, someone else will."

"I'll protect her," I promise him. "Just tell me what's going on and we can stop it."

"You'll protect her?" He sneers at me. "Just like you protected your mom and sister?"

His words pierce my lungs like a knife and I find myself struggling to breathe.

"How can you say that?" Sadie jumps to my defense. "Don't go back to being an asshole, Micah. I liked the new you a lot better."

"Apparently, you didn't like me enough," he mutters, giving me another angry look, and finally, I think I'm starting to understand.

Does he have feelings for Sadie?

"Micah, I had no idea," I tell him honestly. With the way he acted towards her when she first arrived, if he *does* like her, he did a damn good job of hiding it.

My sympathy only seems to make him angrier. "We don't have time for this. You need to get me and Sadie out of the house, now."

"Out?" I repeat, confused all over again. "Where?"

"I'll take her somewhere safe until you can take care of the traitors. Hurry, he'll be here any minute."

I still don't totally understand, but I trust that, even as angry as he is, Micah won't do anything to hurt Sadie, or me, or the pack. I know he's a good guy, deep down, so I'm going to have to trust him.

"This way," I command, gesturing towards a hidden door in the corner of my room. Sadie takes a step, but her dress is still undone, so I stop her and do it back up. She blushes as my fingers brush against her skin, and Micah's jaw clenches again as he watches us.

"Hurry up," he growls again.

We go through the door and into the small space between the walls of the pack house. We always had a couple of escape routes, and after the attack on my mom and Kara last year, my dad had them reinforced and a couple of new ones added. I lead them through the maze of corridors until we end up at a door to the outside.

"The party's still going on," I remind them both. "Try to stay out of sight. Do you know where you're going?"

Micah nods. "I have a plan. They shouldn't be able to find us for a while, so it'll give you some breathing room."

"Who's they?" I ask again, and this time, he finally answers me, but never in a million years could I have expected the answer he gives.

"It's my dad. He's the bastard behind all of it. He's the one after Sadie, and he was the one who ordered the attack on your mom and Kara too. It's been him the whole time."

~~**Sadie's PoV**~~

I see the shock and anger in Logan's eyes as Micah tells us his dad is behind everything. He obviously has a lot of questions and I do too, namely about why Beta Aldric wants me dead in the first place, but there isn't time, and Logan recognizes that too.

"Stay safe," he tells us both grimly. "I'll take care of things here."

Micah nods and opens the door slowly, peering out in both directions before grabbing my hand. "Come on," he says, pulling me along. I shoot one last apologetic look back at Logan before I follow Micah out the door.

Micah hasn't made eye contact with me since he arrived, and I'm burning with guilt and embarrassment. Not that Logan and I were doing anything wrong, but I never wanted Micah to just walk in on us like that. I promised him I'd think about how I felt about him, and instead, he found me making out with his best friend. I don't blame him for being hurt, and I don't know what I can say to make it better.

It's a good thing he doesn't want me to say anything right now anyway. We stay quiet as we sneak across the grounds, staying out of sight of the people still dancing and eating and drinking at Logan's party. I catch sight of Aaron and Laurel, off in the trees by themselves, but luckily, they're so caught up in each other they don't seem to notice us.

It's not until we're out of sight and earshot of the party that Micah turns to me. "We're going to have to move faster than we can go on foot," he says, still not meeting my eye. "I'm going to shift and carry you the rest of the way."

Carry me? As a wolf? I must look shocked because he smirks a little, looking more like himself.

"Just trust me, okay?"

I do trust him, way more than I ever thought I would a couple of weeks ago. So, I turn my back as he strips down and shifts, and when his wolf comes to stand next to me, he's bigger than I realized. He's a deep grey colour, but his eyes are still like Micah's eyes. He gestures with his head towards his back, and, feeling strange about the whole thing, I climb on top of him, lying face down with my hands around his neck.

I'm worried he'll buckle beneath my weight, but he doesn't. He feels strong and stable as he starts to move forward, carrying me on his back, and soon, he starts to run. I gasp in surprise, tightening my grip on Micah's neck, but as he keeps going, the wind rushes through my hair and I smell the forest around us, and suddenly, I feel completely comfortable.

Like this is where I'm meant to be.

Beneath the full moon, in the forest on the back of a wolf, for the first time in a really long time, I feel at home.

It makes no sense, but it's true all the same.

I lose track of time as Micah runs through the forest, never putting a foot wrong, until we arrive at a small, abandoned-looking house deep in the trees. Micah slows to a trot and stops completely outside the front door. I slide off of him as gracefully as I can, still wearing my party dress and heels.

He gestures again with his head, towards the door, and I reach for the handle. It's unlocked, so I let us both in and Micah heads down the hall into a back room. I'm not sure if I'm supposed to follow, so I stay put, looking around the entrance space.

It's cold and dark, but it's not as dirty as I would have expected from the outside. There's a couch and a couple of chairs, and a wood-burning stove. On one side of the room is a small kitchen. It looks like someone might have lived here, a long time ago, but it doesn't look like anyone's been here for a while.

Micah's back a minute later, as a human. He found some pants from somewhere, I guess that's why he went to the back room, but his chest is bare. He's got tattoos I've never seen before, one across the right side of his chest and another one on his left arm. I can just barely make them out in the dim moonlight.

"There's no electricity," he explains, still not looking at me. "There are some candles, but I don't want to risk anyone seeing the light. It'll be better if we don't use them."

"So, we can't have a fire?" I ask as a shiver snakes through my body. It feels colder in here than it did outside, and my dress doesn't cover all that much of me.

Micah's eyes look down my body as his lips tighten. "I'll get you a blanket," he says, going back to the other room again. I sit down on the couch and wait for him to get back and when he returns, he hands me a blanket and keeps one for himself too. He sits down on one of the chairs, far away from me.

For a minute, there's awkward silence, and it's making me crazy. Who knows how long we're going to be here? We're going to have to talk to each other eventually.

"How did you find out it was your dad?" I ask, figuring that's the safest topic to start with.

Micah tells me the whole story, how his dad came to the bar in the city and brought him back to kill me. When he tells me that his dad caused my parent's accident too, I cover my mouth with my hand, and for the first time, he glances over at me, his eyes softening a little bit.

"I had no idea," he says apologetically.

"I know." I believe him completely.

When he gets to the end of the story, we both fall silent again. I know we have to talk about me and Logan, but I'm not sure how to start. I decide to bring up his name first and see what he does.

"Are you in contact with Logan now?" I'm honestly not sure how all this telepathic communication stuff works, but since Logan got his wolf today, I think he can do it too now.

"No," Micah says. "I closed my link so no one can contact me. It's safer that way. My dad might be able to use it to find us."

I guess that makes sense, but then, how will we know what's going on?

"I'll give it some time," he continues, answering my question before I can ask it. "Then I'll check in with him."

It's hard to sit here, not knowing what's going on. My aunt and uncle are probably getting worried about me if they can't find me, and that's assuming all hell didn't break loose when we left. It might have. Literally anything could be happening, and we'd have no idea.

"How long have you and Logan been seeing each other?" he asks, finally addressing the elephant in the room as the bitterness creeps back into his voice.

"We're not exactly seeing each other," I answer truthfully. "We kissed once before, and then... well, tonight happened."

"But you like him?" It looks like it pains him to ask, but he can't help himself.

I can't lie to him either. "Yeah, I do."

"Because he's going to be Alpha?" That question isn't as bitter. He just sounds hurt and a bit confused, like he's trying to understand.

"I don't care about that," I explain as gently as I can. "I like him because he's a good guy."

"And I'm not."

The words are so soft, I almost don't hear them. He looks so sad and lost right now, and it hurts me to see him this way.

"That's not true," I argue. "Micah, you *are* a good person. You're trying to be, anyway, and that's what's important. It's all anyone can do."

"So then, what is it?" he asks, finally looking straight and deep into my eyes for the first time since he showed up tonight. "Why are you choosing him over me?"

I don't know how to explain it to him. I barely know how to explain it to myself. "There's just something there between us," I tell him. "Like a spark."

"A mate spark?" he asks, still looking confused. "But you don't even have your wolf yet."

"I don't know what a mate spark feels like," I tell him. "But the way I feel with Logan is just different. It's nothing that he did, or that you did. It's just how I feel."

He takes a moment to think that over. "And what if you're my mate?" he finally asks when he's done thinking. "If the mate bond gets fixed and you get your wolf, and she tells you I'm your mate, would you reject me then?"

"That's a lot of ifs," I point out. "And I've never liked the idea of anyone telling me who I have to be with. I want to choose for myself."

He almost smiles at that. "That's one of the things I like about you," he admits. "You won't let anyone else tell you what to do."

I don't know how to answer that, and another minute of silence passes before Micah speaks again.

"Logan wants his mate," he tells me. "He won't go against the bond, not when it comes down to it. He'll do what the moon goddess and the pack expect him to."

I know he's right. That's exactly what I've been afraid of.

"But I don't care about that," he continues, leaning forward in his seat to look at me seriously. "If you chose me, Sadie, I would choose you over everything. If Logan can't say the same, then maybe he isn't the right guy for you after all."

~~**Aaron's PoV**~~

Laurel's kiss makes me feel drunk as we make out in the trees behind the pack house. Ever since we marked each other, every sensation is stronger, every touch better.

Our parents weren't entirely pleased about us taking matters into our own hands. We had to meet with them and the Alpha the morning after it happened to explain ourselves. But I told them all that I love Laurel, that I've loved her for years, and that I know in my heart she was meant to be my mate. Maybe the mix-up with the mate bonds would be fixed and maybe it wouldn't, but I couldn't put my life on hold when all I had ever wanted was to be with this amazing woman for the rest of my life.

There was nothing they could say about that.

A movement in the trees catches my attention from the corner of my eyes, and I look over to see Sadie and what looks like Micah Geary running off into the forest. That's more than a little strange. Micah left the pack, everyone knows that. Why would he be back here now?

I'm just about to link to my dad to let him know what I think I saw when a loud howl sounds, drowning out the music of the party and everything else.

It sounds like a call to attack.

We immediately receive a mind-link, to the whole pack, from Logan. I'm impressed he can link the whole pack on his first night as a wolf. It took me a good week before I could consistently do it with even one person.

But his message is not a good one. In fact, it's alarming.

Westbridge is under attack. Beta Aldric has betrayed us all. Warriors, to your positions; everyone else, find shelter.

Laurel and I look at each other in shock. The Beta? That can't be true. He's the pack's staunchest defender. What would he have to gain from betraying us?

More howls fill the air, along with some shouts as people scramble for shelter. I kiss Laurel one last time, hard, and we run back to the party. "Go with the others," I tell her. "Get somewhere safe."

She shakes her head at me furiously. "No way, I'm fighting too."

"Laurel..."

"I'm a warrior too," she reminds me. "Not just your mate."

I know she's right, but the idea of her fighting fills me with fear.

Another link comes through, this time from the Beta himself.

Logan has been fed false information. I assure you, there's no danger. Remain calm and return to your homes. There's no need to assemble.

Everyone looks at each other in confusion. What are we supposed to believe?

Logan is quickly back in our heads again.

Ignore everything he just said. Secure the house and yourselves. Don't let the Beta leave. If anyone finds him, link me immediately.

When the Beta links again, he sounds frustrated.

Apparently, gaining his wolf has affected Logan's mental state. If you see him, secure him for me. I don't want him to hurt himself. I repeat, there is no danger.

This is completely unprecedented and no one knows how to behave. Whose word bears more weight, the Beta or the son of the Alpha? Where is the Alpha himself?

Confusion ripples through the whole party, but people do start to disperse, heading for their homes.

"Should we go too?" Laurel asks.

On the surface, it's a good idea, but something makes me hesitate.

"There's something very odd going on," I tell her. "I need to find Logan. Could you take Ava home?"

I almost expect an argument, but to my surprise, Laurel agrees. She goes to find my sister and I head into the house.

Logan? I reach out to him in my head. *It's Aaron. Where are you?*

He must be dealing with a lot of links at once because he doesn't immediately answer me. I keep trying to reach him as I search the ground floor. Lots of other people are doing the same, but whether they're looking for Logan or for the Beta, I can't be sure.

Finally, he answers me. *Do you have him? Beta Aldric?*

No, I apologize. *I haven't seen him. What's going on? Where are you?*

It takes him another minute to reply. *I'm just getting back to my room. Have you seen my dad?*

I haven't, but I run up the stairs to Logan's room just as he opens the door and comes out.

"What's going on?" is the first question out of my mouth, repeating what I already asked him through the link. "It's chaos downstairs."

"I don't know where the Alpha is," Logan replies grimly. "He's not answering my link."

He heads further down the hall, to his father's office.

"I need him to cut off the Beta's link," he says as he opens the door. "He needs to tell everyone that..."

He trails off as he looks into the room, his face turning white as a sheet, and I quickly go in to look over his shoulder.

The lights are all on and the Alpha is sitting in his chair, his head back and his eyes closed.

His chest is covered in blood.

Chapter Eighteen

~~Logan's PoV~~

For a moment, staring at my dad's limp body in his office chair, all I can see is my mother and my sister when I woke up in that basement and found them both dead. Now, I know it was Beta Aldric who ordered them killed, and I know it's him who did this to my father too. There's not a doubt in my mind.

We need a doctor in the Alpha's office, now!

Aaron's voice rings in my head as he puts out an alert to the whole pack, but I'm still frozen to the spot. It's like I've forgotten how to breathe, or move, or do anything other than stare at the blood on my dad's chest.

He can't be gone. I still need him. The pack still needs him. I can't do this on my own.

One more thought comes into my head: I wish Sadie was here.

As soon as she crosses my mind, I feel a bit calmer and stronger, almost like she's right there beside me. She lost both her parents and had her whole world turned upside down, and she's making the best of it. I draw my inspiration from that as I manage to swallow, and take a breath, and finally, I'm moving over to my dad's chair before I even realize I'm doing it.

"Dad?" There's still some colour in his cheeks, and I feel a small spark of hope. His eyes are still closed, so I put my fingers on his neck, checking for a pulse, and relief floods through me when I feel it beneath my fingertips. It's weak, but it's there.

He's not dead, or at least not yet. *Thank the goddess.*

The pack's doctor comes rushing in the door a few seconds later, followed by other members of my dad's team. When they see their Alpha's lifeless-looking body, they all look just as shocked as I feel.

"What happened?" one of them asks.

"Beta Aldric happened," I growl. "Didn't you hear my message? He's a snake! He wants to overthrow all of us."

They all look at each other with a combination of guilt and confusion and suspicion. "We did hear your announcement,, but we heard the Beta's message too," another one answers me cautiously. "How do we know it was him who did this and not you? If you wanted to take power, you could have tried to throw blame at the Beta first."

Is he fucking kidding me? How could anyone think I would try to kill my own father?

I growl, ready to shift and tear him apart now for even saying such a thing, but Aaron holds me back. "Let's stay calm," he urges me. "We need to get to the bottom of this, and we need to work together."

That's true. Fighting amongst ourselves isn't going to help anyone. I have to rally those loyal to me and make sure that the pack is safe.

I have to make sure that Sadie is safe. Wherever the Beta has gone, I'm certain he's looking for her.

I have no idea where Micah took her, but I hope it's somewhere far away and secure. His words come back to me, the ones he said to me in my room, asking how I could protect her when I couldn't even protect my own family.

It turns out I couldn't protect my dad either.

Maybe he's right. Maybe I'm not cut out for this after all.

My dad groans, and immediately my attention is back on him. "Dad?"

There's no response, so I try again.

"I need you to tell everyone what happened," I beg him. "Tell them who did this to you. They won't believe me."

His eyes flicker open for just a brief moment, but I see them going dimmer, and they close again.

"He's lost a lot of blood," the doctor tells me. "He should be able to heal, but we need to get him a transfusion. He won't be able to talk to you, or to anyone, for a couple of hours."

A mix of emotions runs through me. First is relief that he's going to be okay. They'll treat him and he'll be fine. He's strong and a good healer.

But I'm also frustrated. Without my dad to back me up, how do I get everyone to believe me? Linking the pack obviously didn't work.

As I cast about in my mind for a solution, something occurs to me. Maybe I'm going about this wrong. Maybe I need to start smaller.

I think about how Sadie came up to me that day in the cafeteria, talking to me when everybody else had given up on me. It was a small thing, just one person talking to another, but it started a chain reaction that led me here, back to my rightful place within the pack.

Maybe, somehow, I could do the same.

This is what I was born for. It's time to take my place, once and for all.

"Aaron, you believe me, right?" I turn to the pack member closest to me. "Beta Aldric is behind this. I wouldn't betray my father and my pack this way. I've sworn my life to protect all of us."

He looks straight into my eyes and I hold his gaze, letting my wolf's power and my own latent Alpha authority come through until he bows his head in submission.

"I believe you," he says. "Of course I do. What do we do?"

That's one person, so I turn to the others in the room. "The Beta has betrayed all of us," I tell them, keeping my voice measured but firm. They need to see I'm in control. "He's been plotting to take over the pack. He's behind the mix-up with the mates, and now he tried to kill the Alpha. Look in your hearts. Who do you trust to protect this pack more, him or me?"

This time, they don't look away from me. They stand a little straighter instead.

"We trust you, Logan."

That's a few more.

Now, the rest.

~~Micah's PoV~~

Sadie looks at me with those big, beautiful eyes of hers as I ask her to choose me. I know it's a bit of an asshole move. She obviously has feelings for Logan and he must like her too. I've never known him just to fool around with anyone, so if he didn't have some kind of feelings for her, he wouldn't have done it.

But I also know what I said was true. Logan won't go against the mate bond. It would be a bad example for the pack, and his responsibility to the pack means everything to him. More than Sadie does, I'm sure of that.

She deserves someone willing to put her first, and I could give her that.

And besides, if I don't say something now, I might never get another chance.

If she tells me she's not interested, then I'll deal with that, but I have to at least try.

I've never even thought about committing to someone until I met her, but now it sounds natural to say it. She makes me feel something completely new. She makes me want to be better. I don't think it's a coincidence that it was through helping her that I learned exactly how much of my life was built on a lie, trying to emulate a man who was never worth trying to impress.

"What about Blair?" she asks, and the question takes me completely by surprise. To be honest, I haven't thought about Blair in days.

"What about her?"

"She's been missing you," Sadie tells me. "When you left, she was really upset. Aren't you guys sort of seeing each other?"

Blair was missing me? I had no idea. We've hardly spoken since Sadie and I made peace with each other, and I thought it was just as casual for her as it was for me.

"We hooked up a few times," I admit. "That's all it was."

Fuck, this isn't the way I wanted this conversation to go. The last thing I want to do is talk about other girls, especially since I know that it doesn't put me in a good light next to Logan.

"And what about your mate?" she asks next. "It wouldn't bother you that there's somebody out there that you're supposed to be with and you're choosing not to be?"

"I've never given it a lot of thought," I answer honestly. "I figured it would happen when it happened but it's not like I sit in my room dreaming about it."

That makes her smile.

"And I honestly don't think there could be anyone better for me out there than you are."

"How can you be so sure?" Her question is curious and sincere, and she leans forward in anticipation of my answer.

"Because you're special." It's the best way I can explain it. "You're different, Sadie. At first I thought it was a bad kind of different, as you know."

She smiles again, her eyes warm. She's obviously forgiven me for how much of a jerk I was, which is just another reason I admire her.

"But the more I got to know you, the more I realized it's an amazing different. And I think we could be amazing together, if you gave it a chance."

I get up, leaving the chair I'm in, and go sit next to her on the couch. She doesn't move back, she just keeps watching me curiously.

"You don't need to decide right this second," I say. I don't want to put pressure on her, I just want her to know she's got options. "But before you make any decisions, you should have all the information."

Sitting this close to her, I can see the lighter brown flecks in her dark brown eyes. She's looking at me too, really looking at me, more than she's ever done before.

"And maybe..." I suggest, leaning a bit closer. "You need a bit more information so you can make a direct comparison."

When our lips meet this time, it's a lot better than it was the first time. She's expecting it, for one thing, and there's a new desperation in me too. This is my one chance to prove to her that whatever connection she's got with Logan, we've got our own chemistry too.

I'm not going to waste my chance.

My hand goes around the back of her head, holding her firmly as I take the kiss deeper. She tastes as good as I could have imagined, like sunshine and hope and promises. Like all my favorite things rolled into one.

And she kisses me back too. Maybe not with quite as much passion as I'm kissing her, but she's giving it a chance, and it's good. I can see just how good it would be to get to kiss her every day.

Suddenly, there's a bright flash of light, so bright that I see it clearly through my closed eyelids. We break apart in surprise, both turning towards the source of the light, and my mouth drops open when I see the figure standing there.

It's a woman, a beautiful woman, standing in the middle of the room even though the door never opened. She's bathed in light, but not a bright light anymore after that initial burst. It's more subtle, just a gentle glow.

Like moonlight.

Her eyes rest on me for just a second before moving to Sadie, and she smiles at her with an expression full of kindness and tenderness.

"Hello, Sadie," she says. "I know I'm a few days early, but your wolf has been calling to me. It seems you've all gotten in a bit of trouble here and could use some help."

Her wolf? I look at Sadie in surprise, but she looks as confused as I am. How could her wolf be doing anything yet when she hasn't turned 18 yet?

"Who are you?" Sadie asks the woman, and I think she genuinely doesn't know.

I know, though. My wolf is already on his knees in my mind, bowing to the creator of us all.

The Moon Goddess herself.

~~**Sadie's PoV**~~

Micah looks at me in surprise when I ask the woman who she is, but I don't understand his confusion. It's a perfectly reasonable question considering she just showed up out of nowhere and knows my name. And why is she talking about my wolf? I thought I wouldn't get a wolf until I turn 18, though I confess I still don't fully understand how it all works.

The woman doesn't answer me right away. She smiles at Micah instead. "Micah, would you give me and Sadie a moment to speak alone?"

She knows his name too, but he doesn't seem bothered by that fact. He immediately gets to his feet, not even asking me if I want to be left alone with this stranger. "Of course," he tells her, bowing his head. "Please tell me if there's any way I can help."

"I will."

He gives me a quick smile too before leaving the room, and I'm more confused than ever, not just about this unexpected visitor, but about everything that just happened between Micah and me too.

The kiss was really nice, actually. A lot better than the kiss he gave me outside my house. He's being open and honest with me about how he feels, and I really appreciate that. I know he was hurt to find me and Logan together that way, but he didn't lash out or get angry with me. He just stated his case plainly and asked me to think about it. And thinking about it, there are a lot of things I like about Micah. He's brave and loyal and funny, and I'd have to be blind not to find him attractive physically.

If it weren't for the way I feel about Logan, I could imagine being with Micah, I really could. But Logan is still there, or at least the hope of him is. But even though he'd been ready to give me more tonight, I know that Micah has a point about the long term. If Logan and I aren't mates, will he still want to be with me? I can't be sure, and that breaks my heart a little bit.

I wish there was a way to combine all their best features into one person, and that would be my dream guy, no question. But that's hardly fair to either of them.

Anyway, it's not the time for thinking about that now, so I push all that aside to focus on the woman in front of me, who comes and sits down on the couch beside me now in the seat that Micah just left.

"This is not how I hoped we would meet," she says, her elegant voice almost like music. "I'm very sorry about your parents."

"Who are you?" I repeat, getting frustrated that she won't just answer me. How does she know me and how does she know about my parents?

She looks amused by the question. "My name is Selene, but most people simply call me the Moon Goddess."

My eyes widen as I look at her again. The pale glow surrounding her does seem unworldly, but I'm still not even sure I believe in goddesses. How could there be one sitting on the couch next to me?

"Why are you here?" I blurt out.

"I'm here because you are my vessel," she explains. "There are hundreds of thousands of vessels in the werewolf world. The number of wolves continues to multiply, which is a great blessing. But I cannot be everywhere at once, which is why my power has been delegated."

"But why are you here *now*?" I ask, still not understanding.

"I'm here because of the danger you're in," she says with sorrow in her eyes. "I didn't know anything had happened to the other vessels until your wolf called to me."

Again with the wolf. "I don't have a wolf," I tell her. "At least not yet."

A small smile crosses her face. "That's not quite true. She is in you, she just hasn't revealed herself to you yet. She has been a part of you since the day you were born."

"So she can talk to you, but not to me?" I still don't understand.

"In a way," she says. "She has been praying to me, asking for my help, and somehow, it broke through all the other millions of prayers that come to me every day. I heard her clearly, and so I'm here to help. Why don't you tell me exactly what's going on?"

I suppose I can do that. I tell her everything, all about Logan's mother and sister and how they died, about my own parents and about everything that had happened since I got to the pack, all of the mate mix-up and the people trying to kill me. Every last part of it.

When I finally finish, she nods her head in understanding. "It hurts me when any of my children behave the way that Beta Aldric has," she tells me, and I believe her. I can hear the sorrow in her voice.

"Can you stop him?" I ask.

She shakes her head. "I can't directly interfere. Just as there are rules that govern your world, Sadie, there are laws that restrict me too. I have to trust my children to sort things out themselves, using their own free will."

Free will? I'm surprised when she uses those words. "But you determine who they are going to love," I point out. "Isn't that interfering?"

"That's not what I do," she corrects me gently. "I make it so you can recognize the person who is right for you. Your souls are made for each other, I just place the markers to help you find each other. It's not random. Each mate is still individually chosen based on each wolf's personality and needs. Sometimes I get it wrong, but not often."

"So, if you can't interfere, then why are you here?" It doesn't make sense to me.

"I've come to establish you fully as my vessel. I will bring your wolf forward now, tonight, so that you can receive my power and the mate situation will be fixed. You will still need to defeat the Beta on your own, but once you have your wolf, you can communicate with the pack and tell them what you know. You'll also be able to defend yourself better, should the need arise. It should all be a help to you."

That does sound helpful. It's better than nothing, anyway. But am I really ready to become a full werewolf tonight? There's still so much I don't know, even without taking the whole vessel business into consideration.

As if she's read my thoughts, Selene leans closer to me, looking straight into my eyes. "What do you think, Sadie? Are you ready to claim your wolf?"

Chapter Nineteen

~~Logan's PoV~~

My father's team is assembled on the lawn, all listening to me. Following my new plan, I spoke to people one-on-one and they started speaking to others, and now, I have a big group ready to fight with me. There are a few important people missing, senior members of our security forces, and I have to guess that they are with Beta Aldric. I couldn't have guessed that we had that many traitors in our ranks, and I know my dad will be heartbroken when he learns of their betrayal.

I've sent a small team to the hospital to keep watch over my dad and make sure that no one gets to him. I wouldn't put it past the Beta to try to attack him again once he learns he failed to kill him. With that done, I focus the rest of the group on finding Aldric and bringing him to justice once and for all.

"He's looking for Sadie Jennings," I tell them all, my voice carrying across the open air. "He believes that by killing her, the Moon Goddess' influence will be broken and all mate bonds will break with it. That will allow him and his forces to take advantage of the resulting chaos and take over not only Westbridge but the other packs in the area too."

I see surprise on their faces as I lay out his plan, but no signs of disbelief.

"He was behind the attack that killed the Luna and Kara as well," I tell them, wanting them to have all the information. "He's betrayed all of us. If you need to use deadly force against him or anyone who is fighting with him, you have my permission. I will answer to the Alpha for it."

Again, there is no argument. I have their trust now, I can feel it, and it makes me stronger.

I reach out in my mind for Micah again, hoping he has reopened his link, but there's still no reply. I wish I knew where they were, but on the other hand, it's more important that we find the Beta. For now, we need to focus on tracking him.

When I give the order, the team breaks up into smaller search groups that will spread out across the territory. Aaron is still there, and I see that Laurel and Ava have come back too. Ava catches my eye as I walk past.

"Is Sadie okay, Logan?" The worry in her voice is the same as what's in my heart.

"She was the last time I saw her," I answer honestly. "Micah promised to protect her."

That seems to make her feel better. "I know he'll do his best," she says, and I have to agree with that. He won't let any harm come to her if there's anything he can do about it.

With our teams formed, I tell everyone to head out and we all shift and spread out into the woods, leaving a small group to guard the pack house as well in case the Beta comes back. The moon shines down on us and I send up a silent prayer to the Moon Goddess, asking her to help me protect my pack and to keep Sadie safe.

I hope she can hear me.

~~Ava's PoV~~

I'm in the same group with Laurel and Aaron. It wasn't on purpose, it's just the way it worked out, but I'm glad to have them nearby anyway. I know they're as anxious about Sadie as I am.

I can't believe all of this, that Sadie is the vessel and that's why her parents were killed, or that it was the Beta who's behind it all. But yet, I do believe it, because Logan said it's true, and I know he wouldn't lie to us. This pack means everything to him.

A wolf howls in the distance and our squad leader stops, his ears twitching to identify the direction the sound came from. A couple of seconds later, he takes off and we all follow in behind.

We've only had a couple of weeks of training with our wolves and I wasn't expecting to be involved in any kind of real fighting so soon, but I'm ready for it anyway. Just like Logan, my responsibility is to the pack now.

And maybe, I can't help thinking, if we get this all taken care of tonight, the mate bond will be restored and I can find my real mate after all. That would be really nice.

The smell of other wolves grows stronger as we get deeper into the woods. They're from our pack, but at the moment, I know that doesn't count for much. They could be from our pack and still be enemies. It's civil war.

Although we're quiet, they must have smelled us too, because suddenly we're ambushed out of nowhere. The wolf in front of me is taken down and his throat ripped out in a matter of seconds, and my heart nearly stops.

Ava, move!

That's Aaron in my head, and I realize I've frozen to the spot, watching my packmate bleed out in front of me. I've never seen anyone die before, not like this at least, but there's no time to mourn. We're still under attack.

I jump on the back of the wolf who just killed my squad mate. He howls as my claws dig into him and he tries to throw me off. I don't know who he is, but he must be someone I've gone to parties with, that I've seen at picnics and other pack meetings. How have we come to this?

I cling on as best as I can until Laurel appears in front of us and joins in the fight. Together, we manage to bring him down and Laurel uses her strong jaws to break his back legs. She doesn't kill him though.

It's not the Beta, she tells me by mind-link. *Leave him for now.*

The other wolves who attacked us have all been subdued as well, and we leave them there, injured but not dead, as we carry on deeper into the forest.

~~Sadie's PoV~~

Selene's question is still ringing in my head: am I ready for this?

I'm not entirely sure, but I also know that I don't have much choice. If I can help Logan and the others by claiming my wolf now, then I have to do it.

I guess I do care about the pack too, when it comes down to it. I'm part of something bigger than myself, and there's a responsibility that comes with that.

For the first time, I can truly see where Logan is coming from.

"I'm ready," I tell her.

She smiles once more. "This is going to feel a bit strange," she warns me before placing the tips of her fingers on my temples.

Light flashes in front of my eyes and I close them instinctively, but I can still see the light behind my eyelids. A strange warmth fills my body, and then, quietly at first, but growing louder bit by bit, I hear a new sound in my head.

A new voice.

Sadie? I'm Ebony, your wolf.

I'm not sure if I'm meant to answer, so I don't say anything, and a few seconds later she tries again.

Can you hear me?

I suppose I better reply, though it feels very weird to talk to someone that only exists in my head. *I hear you.*

I feel her joy inside me, almost like it's my own, but not exactly the same. What an odd sensation. I suddenly have a new appreciation for how Ava must have felt when her wolf was sad and angry with her about the whole situation with her mate.

This is going to take some getting used to, I tell her wryly.

I know, she assures me. *But we'll figure it out together. We're a team now, Sadie.*

I open my eyes again and Selene is looking at me curiously. "How do you feel?"

"Like I've got a multiple personality disorder?" I say, and she laughs.

"You will get used to it, and very quickly too. Soon, you'll wonder how you ever lived without your wolf."

I find that a bit difficult to believe, but I suppose she has been around a lot longer than I have. Maybe she knows what she's talking about.

"Do I have your power now, then?" I ask her.

Selene nods. "I transferred it to your wolf when I called her forward. As soon as you shift for the first time, you will fully inherit it."

Shift? I guess I was going to have to turn into a wolf, just like I'd seen everyone else do. For a brief moment, I really wish my mom was here, but I know I have to be brave and do this for her sake too as well as everyone else's. The man who's responsible for her death is still out there. I can't let him win.

"There is one other gift I want to give you before I go," Selene says, taking hold of my hands. Her hands are cool, like the night air.

"A gift?" I repeat. "For me?"

"Ebony has told me that you have doubts about the whole mate process," she explains with a knowing smile. "That you doubt that I can choose the right partner for you."

It's a bit embarrassing to have the goddess herself know that I doubted her, but I can't deny it either. "I just think that I can make my own choice," I try to explain.

To my surprise, she nods. "I agree with you. You have a fire in you, Sadie. It's kept you strong through everything you've been through, and you will need it to continue in the work you're meant to do. You need a partner who recognizes and appreciates it. I believe I know who that partner should be, but if you want, I will leave the choice to you."

I couldn't be more surprised. "You'll let me decide?"

Once again, she nods. "Whoever you choose, I will place the mate bond between you. If it's who I intended for you, nothing will change. But if you choose someone else, I will change the bond and no one will ever know the difference. If you truly want the responsibility, I will give it to you, as my thanks for protecting my children here and carrying on my legacy."

This is completely unexpected and my mind races as I try to figure out what to do.

If I choose Logan, he will feel the bond between us. He will accept me as his mate because it's what he's meant to do.

But Micah already chose me, regardless of the bond. He wants me no matter what, and a bond between us would only strengthen that.

"Can you tell me who you already chose?" I ask tentatively, and Selene smiles.

"That might influence your choice," she points out. "I will tell you afterwards, if you like. But first, I need you to tell me your choice, Sadie. Who do you want your mate to be?"

~~**Micah's PoV**~~

I'm unable to sit still as I wait in the back bedroom of the old house in the forest. I used to play here all the time when I was a kid, whenever I wanted to get away from my dad. Logan and I had come across the house one day when we were out exploring the forest together and he asked his dad about it. The Alpha told us it used to belong to one of the pack elders who became something of a hermit, who wanted to live alone but still remain on the pack land, but he had died a little while earlier and no one had used it since. He said Logan and I were welcome to use it if we wanted to.

We cleaned it all up and used it as our headquarters for all kinds of elaborate games we made up. Logan and I were inseparable for a long, long time, but we started to drift apart a little bit in high school. I started spending time with lots of different girls, and Logan wasn't interested in casual flirting or hook-ups. We started to have different interests. And then, of course, there was the attack where the Luna and Kara were killed, and everything changed for Logan.

Looking around the room, remembering all the times we had here, I think maybe I could have been a better friend to him during the last year. He pushed me away, yeah, but he was hurting, and I knew that. Maybe I should have fought harder. He let Sadie in, after all. Maybe he would have let me in too if I had tried a little more and thought a little less about myself.

Or maybe it was really her he needed her all along.

Over the last few weeks, Sadie has brought us closer together again, more like how we used to be, but she's pulling us apart too, though not on purpose.

I know she makes me want to be better and I guess she does that for Logan too. But we can't both have her. I'm not interested in sharing, and I'm sure Logan isn't either. Sooner or later, she's going to have to choose, and I can only hope that I've done enough that she'll consider me.

I pace around the room like a caged animal, waiting for Sadie or the Goddess to call me back, until I realize there is something useful I could be doing instead, so I open my link to the pack and reach out to Logan.

Micah? He sounds relieved to hear me, but also out of breath, which is weird, since he's not actually using his lungs to speak to me right now. *Are you safe? Where's Sadie?*

We're safe, I assure him. *She's still with me and no one's found us.*

Where are you? He sounds a bit distracted, and I can't contain my curiosity.

What's going on? Have you got my dad yet?

Not exactly, he admits. *I'm working on it. Where are you?*

The old elder's house in the woods.

I almost hear his sigh of relief. *That's perfect. Stay there, I'll send a squad to stand guard.*

Stand guard? *So, they're still looking for her?*

Sorry, Micah, I have to go. He closes the link before I can get an answer.

Shit. It doesn't sound like things are going very well. I wish I could go out and help, but I know it's more important that I stay here and make sure Sadie's protected.

And now that I know she might still be in danger, I can't wait any longer. I open the door to the room and head back out to the living room. The Moon Goddess is sitting next to Sadie on the couch now, like they're friends, just talking to her. They both look at me in surprise when I come in, and I feel like I've interrupted something.

"I'm sorry," I apologize to them both. "I just wanted to make sure everything was okay, I've heard that the people looking for Sadie are still out there. I needed to see that she was safe."

The Goddess gets to her feet and Sadie quickly follows. "You should focus on helping your pack," she tells Sadie. "Once that's finished, I will return and you can give me your answer then. Until then, you won't feel a bond with anyone, whether they are fated for you or not."

There's another flash of light and I close my eyes against it. When I open them again, the Goddess is gone. Only Sadie and I are left in the room.

"What was all that about?" I ask curiously.

"It's a long story," Sadie says, looking conflicted before she gives her head a shake. "But Selene is right, we need to help the others now."

"Selene?" She's on a first name basis with the Moon Goddess now?

Sadie shrugs. "I guess. But listen, Micah, I've got my wolf now."

She does? "So... you can recognize your mate?" I ask hesitantly. If that's the case, it's not me. I would have known it the second I walked in, and a lump fills my throat at the idea that I've missed my chance after all.

But Sadie shakes her head. "Not yet. Like I said, it's a long story. But I've got other abilities now, apparently, and I need to use them to stop your father."

That's definitely my goal too. "What do you want to do?" I ask her.

She looks at me with a new fire in her eyes. "I want to fight."

Chapter Twenty

~~Logan's PoV~~

I'm glad I know where Sadie and Micah are, and as soon as he told me where he'd taken her, I saw just how smart it was. I don't think anyone knows about that place besides us. It was forgotten a long time ago, and since Beta Aldric never cared much about what his son did, he probably never even knew that we used to play there, not like my dad did.

It's about the only good news I have right now though. I keep getting reports of casualties. Obviously, the Beta knows we're tracking him, so he's started setting his people to attack us. I can't believe these are our friends, our packmates, all turned against us, and for what? To take control of the pack and stop us mingling with humans? It all seems so petty and pointless to me, but they're not going to get away with it.

I won't let them.

I'm just about to link with the group that Aaron and Ava went with to tell them to head over to the house, since they're closest to it, when a new voice echoes in my head.

Logan? Are you there?

The voice takes me by surprise, but I know for sure whose voice it is. *Sadie? How are you linking to me?*

It's a long story, she answers, sounding a little exasperated, like she's said it before. *We're coming to you now though, me and Micah. Where are you?*

That wasn't the plan. *No, you need to stay there. I'm sending people to protect you.*

And who's going to protect you?

It's a sweet question, but not the point. *I'm not the one people are trying to kill right now.*

"I wouldn't be so sure about that."

Those words are spoken out loud, and I turn around in shock to find the person who spoke them.

Beta Aldric stands behind me, in his human form, with wolves on either side of him. My small group instantly flanks me, forming a standoff in the middle of the woods.

We'd be pretty evenly matched if this was a fair fight, but I already know enough about the Beta to know that whatever he's got planned, it's going to be cowardly and underhanded.

How did you hear my conversation with Sadie? I ask him, speaking to him in my head since I'm still in my wolf form. Sadie and I were talking by mind-link too, and it should have been private.

"She linked the whole pack," Aldric sneered, speaking aloud again so everyone could hear him, and I quickly turned to one of my wolves next to me to see if that was true. He nods back at me to say he heard it too.

Really? I don't understand how Sadie could link me at all, never mind link the whole pack. Usually only the highest-ranked wolves can do that. And obviously she didn't mean to, she wouldn't have wanted to give anything away.

In any case, it's not my biggest worry right now. I look over the snarling, growling wolves next to the Beta, trying to figure out what his plan is.

He quickly answers for me. "Tell me where she is, Logan. If you do, I'll let you live, you and anyone who surrenders with you. You can take them all and go find another pack to live in, far away from here."

I'm not telling you anything, I growl at him in my head.

Aldric shrugs. "That's your choice, but if you don't, I'll kill everyone who supported you. I'll make you watch them die, just like your mother and sister did, with you knowing that you could have saved them. And then I'll kill you too."

As I stare at him in disbelief, I can't believe we never knew just what a sick piece of shit he really is. How can he stand there and talk to me about my mom and Kara when he's the one who ordered their deaths?

I'm going to tear you apart, one piece at a time, I reply, staring at him with more hatred than I've ever felt for anyone. *You're going to beg for mercy, beg for death, and I'll laugh in your face.*

He laughs instead. "That's cute, Logan, but you don't have the balls for that. You're weak. You're nothing but an afterthought. You were never meant to be Alpha, and you never will be. Now stop stalling and tell me where she is."

"I'm right behind you, you son of a bitch."

None of us heard Sadie approach. She made no sound, gave off no scent. I don't know how it's possible, and obviously, Aldric doesn't either as he spins around in disbelief to see her standing in the trees just a few paces away.

Now! I command my wolves and they spring forward to take out the Beta's backup. Another wolf comes flying out of the trees to join the fray and I recognize Micah. He goes straight for his father, but he's stopped by one of the others. I go to help him, trying to keep my eyes on Sadie as I fight, but there's too much going on. All I can do is keep the wolves away from her and hope that she's got some kind of plan for what to do with Beta Aldric.

~~Sadie's PoV~~

My hand clenches around the handle of the knife in my pocket as Micah's dad's eyes meet mine. I just need him to come a little closer. Micah promised me all I have to do is nick him with the knife, just a scratch, and that will be enough.

I didn't even know that he put the knife in my pocket. He says he did it when he shifted to his wolf in the woods outside the pack house, when I was distracted, because he didn't have anywhere to carry it once he was naked. He told me he was supposed to use it to kill me, that his dad gave it to him for that reason, but that now, I can use it against his father instead. He says it would be poetic justice.

I've never fought anyone before, and certainly not with a deadly weapon. But this man wants to kill me, he killed my parents, and he killed Logan's mom and sister too. If there was ever anyone who deserved to die, it's him, so I'm ready to do what I have to do.

I guess I'm more animal than I realized.

His eyes stay fixed on me in spite of the wolves fighting around him. They glint dangerously beneath the moonlight.

"Apparently, my stupid son couldn't even betray me properly," he says, sounding amused and frustrated at the same time. "He led you straight to me."

"Micah's ten times the man you are," I tell him, tightening my grip on the knife once again. "Which is a miracle considering you're the one who raised him."

He just smiles at me coldly. "And you were raised by a human and a wolf who was pretending to be one. They hid the best part of you from you for all your life. You don't deserve to be the vessel. You don't deserve to be part of this pack at all. And without your wolf, you don't even know how much danger you're in right now."

In a split second, he moves towards me, shifting into his wolf in mid-air. I see him coming, but I don't move. I stay rooted to the spot, waiting for him to be close enough.

Waiting...

Waiting...

At the last second, I pull the knife out of my pocket and hold it out in front of me. His eyes widen as he sees it but there's nothing he can do. He's already airborne, already committed to the attack.

And as he lands on top of me, the knife drives deep into his wolf's chest at the same time his claws dig into my skin, shredding my flesh as blood pours from the wounds.

"Sadie!"

I don't know who shouts it. Maybe it's Logan. Maybe it's Micah. Maybe it's both.

But I can't look to see. My eyes feel heavy, and the last thing I see is the Beta's wolf falling limply to the ground before darkness takes me too.

When I open my eyes again, it's not night anymore. It's bright, but with a strange glow around everything, and when I turn my head, I'm not even surprised to see Selene there. This whole place looks like her. It must be her home.

"Am I dead?" I ask, looking down at my body. There are no wounds, not even scratches. How is that possible?

She smiles and shakes her head. "No. Your body is still there, in the woods, but it needs time to heal. I brought your spirit here so we could finish our talk before you go back."

I'm a spirit? At this point, all I can do is shrug. Why the hell not? It's not even the weirdest thing to happen to me today.

"Did I kill him?" I ask. I don't know if she'll know, but she nods her head.

"Aldric is dead. The pack will be safe, thanks to you, and Logan, and Micah. The three of you make a good team."

We do, but it can't always be the three of us. I need to choose, and that's why I'm here. I understand that without her spelling it out.

I've been thinking about it ever since she left, thinking about it as Micah and I made our way through the woods to find Logan. Micah's sense of smell is good and he could sniff out his father without too much trouble. We ran quietly, trying not to attract attention, and it gave me a bit of time to think.

If I choose Logan and Selene makes him my mate, on the surface, it sounds great. He would feel our bond and would want to be with me. But if he found out that I made the choice, that the bond might have been changed, I don't think he would like it. He might feel like I cheated, or manipulated him somehow, and he might come to resent me, and that's the last thing I want.

On the other hand, if I choose Micah and Selene makes him my mate instead, I don't think he will mind that I made the choice. In fact, he'd probably be happy that I chose him. But what if he has a different mate out there, someone who would be the perfect complement to him, and I get in the way of that? What if she never finds someone else who's as good for her? What if we aren't as good together as he seems certain we will be?

The more I think about it, the more complicated it gets. I can see reasons to choose them both and I can see reasons to not choose them both. And the more I think about it, the more I decide that maybe I don't want that responsibility after all.

I thought I wanted to be free to make the choice, but if I'm going to fully accept being a wolf, if I'm going to be part of the pack and everything that goes with it, then maybe I have to accept that the mate bond is a key piece of that. Maybe, just this once, I have to give up my desire for control and accept the path that's been laid for me.

I didn't ask to be a werewolf, but I am. I didn't ask to be the vessel either, but I'm that too. And if that's my life, if I'm fully going to claim my place as a wolf, maybe I have to claim my full destiny and everything that involves.

So, that's what I tell Selene. That's the choice I make.

"I want you to restore the mate you chose for me. I want you to choose."

She smiles at me like she always knew that's what I'd say. "When you wake up again, he will be there," she promises me. "You'll be my vessel now until your own daughter comes of age, and I will visit her then. Maybe I'll see you again at that time too."

"I would like that," I tell her sincerely. It's actually a bit comforting to know that there is someone watching over us, even some of the time.

"Good luck, Sadie," she whispers, and my eyes start to feel heavy again. Darkness surrounds me, and the next thing I know, I hear several voices above me.

"She's moving!"

"Sadie? Can you hear me?"

Someone's holding my hand, and I feel sparks shooting through me, kind of like the tingles I felt with Logan before, but even stronger.

Mate! Ebony shouts gleefully in my head.

I guess he's here. I guess this is it, the moment that will determine my path for the rest of my life.

With my heart racing, I open my eyes to see who it is.

~~Logan's PoV~~

As soon as the Beta shifts to his wolf and leaps at Sadie, I run towards her. From the corner of my eye, I see Micah do the same. For some reason, she doesn't move or try to get out of the way. She just stands there, waiting for him to attack, and I shift back into my human form to try to warn her, though I don't know how she can miss it.

"Sadie!" I shout just as the Beta lands on her, tackling and pinning her to the ground, and she cries out in pain as his claws rip through her flesh. I almost feel like it's my skin being torn, it hurts me just as much to see her in pain.

Micah's still in his wolf form and he hits his father, pushing him off Sadie, but it's not necessary. The Beta's wolf has gone limp, but I'm not worried about him right now. I rush to Sadie's side just as her eyes close, and it feels like my whole world dims too.

"No!" I shout hoarsely at no one in particular. "Not this time. You can't leave me too."

I'm naked from my shift, and so is everyone else around us, but Sadie is still wearing clothes. Apologizing to her in my head, I rip her shirt off and tear it into smaller pieces, my adrenaline giving me even more strength than usual as I create some makeshift bandages for her wounds.

Micah comes up beside me, in his human form too, and I instruct him to press down on two of the biggest wounds, the ones with the most blood, while I work on the others.

"She'll be okay," he promises me, though his voice shakes a little. "She's got her wolf now, she can heal."

How does she have her wolf? I don't understand, but it's not the question I need answered most right now. "What about him?" I ask, gesturing with my head towards the Beta's body even though I don't take my eyes off Sadie.

"Dead," Micah answers coldly. "Sadie has a poisoned knife, she used it on him."

That's why she just stood there and let him attack her? "You said you were going to protect her," I growl at Micah.

"She can protect herself," he snaps right back at me. "And it was only because he thought she was weak that my dad attacked her himself. If it were you or me, he would have sent one of his followers to do it. He was a coward, right to the end."

He has a point there. I tear my eyes away from Sadie to look over at the Beta's lifeless wolf on the forest floor. I'm glad he's dead, but I'm upset too. I really wanted him to properly pay for what he's done, to suffer as he made others suffer. This quick death seems too good for him, but at least it's finished now. Without their leader, the wolves around us have stopped fighting, and I'm getting reports in my head that others are surrendering too. There will be plenty of work to sort out punishments later.

"She's moving!" Micah calls out beside me, and instantly my eyes are back on Sadie. I'm holding her hand in mine, and Micah's got her other one.

"Sadie? Can you hear me?" Thank the Goddess, it looks like she's okay, but I'll feel so much better when I hear her speak.

And as she starts to stir, something new stirs in me too. It's like a fire that starts in my fingers, the ones holding onto hers, and it shoots up my arm, straight to my heart.

Mate!

I hear my wolf Shadow cry out in joy, but I can hardly believe it. Is this for real? He didn't recognize her before at the party. But she didn't have her wolf then, and apparently now she does? Are the bonds fixed? I'm so confused. Part of me is alive with hope, the other part is trying not to get my hopes up too high.

Sadie's dark eyes open and she looks at Micah first, and then at me. A soft smile plays on her lips, and I'm sure she's feeling it too.

"Logan." She says my name sweetly, and I can't help it. I don't care that I'm naked or that Micah's here or that a half dozen other people are watching us too. I lean down and kiss her, and the same sparks I felt in our hands set fire to our lips too, making the kiss even better than it was before.

And it was pretty damn good before.

"Is this for real?" I whisper to her as I pull back, my eyes searching hers for some clue about what's happening.

She nods as she smiles at me. "Everything's fixed now. Everything's right. This is the way it's supposed to be."

Joy floods through me. Sadie is my mate. The girl who brought me out of my darkness is going to be mine, forever.

I'm so overwhelmed with happiness that I try to kiss her again, but she gently puts her hand on my chest to hold me back. "Just a minute, okay?"

Her eyes move to Micah for a second, and I think I understand. She wants to speak to him. I nod at her and get to my feet, taking a few steps away to address the wolves who are still with us. "The fighting's over. Let's get the injured and the dead to the hospital. Thank you all for your support tonight, it won't be forgotten."

I glance back down at Sadie and Micah, but they're talking quietly and I don't want to interrupt, so I move further away, checking in with the rest of the squads, making sure everything's okay.

For the first time in a really long time, I feel like it is.

Chapter Twenty-One

~~Micah's PoV~~

When Sadie opens her eyes, she looks at me first, and along with my relief that she's okay, there's also hope. Maybe this is the moment when she'll choose me?

But then she looks at Logan and I see the change in her eyes and the way they're drawn together, and when he kisses her, I know it deep in my gut.

She's never going to be mine.

Sadie sends Logan away and I hear him start talking to the others, but I can't make out a word he's saying. I'm staring at Sadie instead, waiting for the rejection I know is coming.

"Logan's my mate," she says simply. "The bonds have been restored and my wolf told me."

It's even worse than I thought. It's not just a matter of her choosing him, though that would be bad enough. The Moon Goddess actually put them together. How can that be, when I feel so strongly about her? It doesn't make sense.

"There must be a reason for it," she adds gently. "Which means that there's a reason that you're meant to be with someone else."

"I thought you didn't believe in all of that," I remind her. "What happened to making your own choice?"

She gives me a sheepish shrug. "I guess I don't know everything after all. The Moon Goddess is definitely real, I can't deny that after tonight. So, I had to accept that maybe she knows what she's doing after all."

I swallow my disappointment. Obviously she's made up her mind, and arguing with her about it isn't going to do me any favors. I might be the loser, but I can be a gracious loser, at least. If there's one thing the past few weeks have taught me is that I can be a better man than my father, and that includes accepting defeat.

I get to my feet and help her up. "You should probably shift," I tell her. "We're a long way from the pack house, it'll be quicker to go in your wolf form."

Her eyes widen. "I don't know how to do that."

"I'll help you." Logan's voice rings out from just behind me, and I turn to face him. He's giving me a slightly uneasy look, like he's not sure how I'm taking the news, so I take a step back.

"Of course. It should be you who shows her. Congratulations to you both."

"Micah..."

He starts to say something, but I don't want his pity. He always had the father I wished I had, and now he's got the mate I wanted too. Even if he is my best friend, I kind of hate him right now. So, before he can finish saying whatever was on the tip of his tongue, I shift back to my wolf and take off back towards the hospital.

There's only one person I want to talk to right now.

When I arrive, there are guards outside the Alpha's room, but they let me in without question. That surprises me, but I'm too focused on what I came here to say to really think about it.

"Micah."

The Alpha is sitting up in his bed, his chest bandaged. He looks pale, but otherwise okay. It's obvious he's going to recover, and I'm really glad.

"I had no idea he was a traitor," I blurt out in greeting. "I would have told you if I'd known. I would never betray the pack like he did."

The Alpha holds up his hand. "I know. Logan linked me, he's explained everything you did. You have my thanks, and the thanks of the whole pack. I've always known you had great potential, and tonight, you lived up to it. I'm proud of you, Micah."

Those are words I've never really heard before, and to my annoyance, tears start to gather in my eyes. This whole night has been a roller coaster of emotions, and it's finally catching up with me.

I need to say what I came here to say before I lose focus.

"Alpha, I'd like to request a transfer to another pack."

It's not a typical request, and he looks appropriately shocked. "What do you mean? Micah, with your father gone, you are my Beta and I'm happy to have you in that role. Nobody blames you for what your father did. It's your actions, not your blood, that define you."

It means a lot to me to hear him say that and to know that he wants me as his Beta. If that were the whole situation, I'd be happy to stay, but it's not. Eventually, Logan will take over, with Sadie as his Luna, and the idea of being around them day after day is more than I can take.

I open my mouth to say so, but he cuts me off again. "It's been a really long night, Micah. Sleep on it. That's an order. You can come see me in the morning, hopefully once I'm out of this place, and if you still want to leave, we can talk about it then."

He looks around the room like it's a prison rather than a state-of-the-art medical facility and I can't help but smile.

And since it's a direct order from my Alpha, I also can't refuse, so I bow my head to him and say good night. Exhaustion hits me as I walk out of the room, all the stress of the last week piling up at once, and suddenly, my bed sounds really good. But as soon as I get out in the hallway, I see a flurry of activity at the far end, new casualties arriving, and I head down to see what's happening.

"Aaron? What's going on?"

He's left behind as the nurses rush whoever he was with into the operating room. There's an odd smell in the air lingering in the air, like oranges and cinnamon.

He looks over at me with haunted eyes. "We got ambushed, just before the ceasefire order came in. It's Laurel and Ava. They're both in pretty bad shape. They can't tell me anything else right now."

"Fuck." There's not much else I can say as I look down the hall where they just went. "I'll wait with you. Come on, let's get some coffee or something."

He gives me a grateful nod and together we head down to the coffee machine, hoping that it won't be long before we find out just how bad things are.

~~**Ava's PoV**~~

I don't know what happened. One minute, we were making our way through the forest, and the next I'm lying on the ground with my brother in his human form above me.

"Shit, Ava." His face is pale and he looks way more serious than usual. "It's going to be okay."

I don't know what he's talking about. Everything feels okay to me. I don't know why I'm on the ground at all, but I feel fine, other than being really sleepy all of a sudden.

"No, come on, Ava, keep your eyes open." I hear him talking to me, but it sounds really far away. "Stay awake, sis. Do it for me, please."

That's the last thing I hear until I open my eyes again. Now, it's a lot brighter. It's so bright that I wince as I try to open my eyes.

I hear voices, but they're not ones I recognize. When I finally get my eyes open, I realize that it's the pack doctor and some of the nurses. They're standing over at the bed next to mine. Nobody's looking at me.

"Excuse me?" I say as politely as I can, but it comes out really croaky. It doesn't seem to matter, though; they all hear me, and a second later, they all rush over.

"Ms Miller," the doctor greets me. His face looks tired. "How do you feel?"

I feel okay, the same as I did before. I don't understand why everyone's looking so serious around me all of a sudden. "I'm fine. Why am I here?"

They all look at each other. "How do your legs feel?" the doctor asks me more specifically.

I frown. Nothing hurts, so I don't know why they're making such a big deal about it, but when I try to move my legs, nothing happens. I try to sit up, but a nurse quickly pushes me back down.

"Not yet, Ava. You need to rest."

"But I can't move my legs," I tell them. "Why can't I?"

A look of understanding passes over the doctor's face, and I don't like it. "Well, that explains one thing," he says. "Try not to worry too much yet, Ms Miller. Your body's still healing and you're young and strong. It's too early to say if any of the damage will be permanent."

"What damage? What's wrong with me?" I'm starting to panic. Why won't he give me a straight answer?

"Ava?"

A new voice sounds from the door, and immediately, my wolf jumps to attention. A new smell fills the air, like leather and sunshine, and as everyone turns to the door, they block my view. I can't see who it is, but my wolf seems to know.

Mate! She shouts joyfully.

I groan internally. Not again. I can't go through another messed-up mate bond, and especially not right now.

But when the person pushes through the crowd to me, I'm surprised to see who it is.

"Micah?"

"It's okay," he says, taking hold of my hand, and instantly, sparks fly up my arm, sending tingles all through my body. His eyes are locked on mine intensely. "I could feel you getting upset, but you don't need to worry. I'm here for you."

He could feel it? But that didn't make sense, unless we really were mates.

But we can't be, can we?

I don't even have to ask him. He seems to be able to read the confusion in my face. "Sadie got her wolf," he explains. "She became the Moon Goddess' vessel, which means the mate bonds are back to how they should be."

"So, you really are my mate?" I ask tentatively. I don't know how he's going to feel about that. Last I heard, he was kissing Sadie, and before that he was with Blair. He's never shown me anything other than friendship before.

But the way he's looking at me now suggests he's not as upset about it as I thought he might be. "It looks like it," he says, giving me a shrug, but there's a smile in his eyes too. "It's been one hell of a night."

I realize I feel calmer with him here, just like I did on the night of my birthday when he helped me shift. Now that I think about it, I've always felt pretty comfortable with Micah. I just never really noticed it before.

"Let's see what's going on with your legs," he says, and he lifts the blanket covering them, despite the protests of the nurses.

They're covered in bandages, most of them soaked through with dried blood. Micah swallows hard as he looks down at them before looking back at me.

"It doesn't hurt?" he asks, and I shake my head no. They look like they should, but I don't feel anything.

The doctor starts to whisper something to him, but he immediately shakes his head.

"Don't tell me, tell her. It's her body."

I appreciate that, and I give him a smile of thanks. He squeezes my hand in support.

"The whole lower half of your body suffered pretty severe injuries, Ms Miller," the doctor says. "There may have been some damage to your spinal cord that's affecting your ability to move your legs and to feel any pain in them. But as I said before, we can't say yet whether it will be permanent."

Panic starts to rise inside me, and immediately, Micah's hand is on my cheek, turning my face to look at him. His eyes are close to me, really close, but a soothing calm flows through me as he looks at me. "Getting upset about it isn't going to change anything," he tells me softly. "Let's give your body a chance to heal and see what happens, okay?"

I nod, and the next thing I know, he's kissing me. It's just a gentle touch of his lips on mine, nothing passionate, but it's sweet and calming, and the tingles on my lips send a shiver through me anyway.

"I guess she was right," I hear him say, almost to himself.

"Who was right?" I ask.

He smiles at me. "Sadie. And the Moon Goddess too. I met her tonight, you know."

I roll my eyes at him, and he laughs.

"Don't believe me if you don't want to, but it's true. You're going to have to learn to trust me, Ava. I only lie when I really need to."

Despite myself, I laugh too. I'm still worried about my legs and everything else, but with Micah here, I feel like maybe it's going to be okay, no matter what happens.

Like he said, this has been one hell of a night.

~~**Aaron's PoV**~~

I was only gone for a few minutes to make a few calls. I had to call my parents and Laurel's parents too, to tell them what was going on, and convince them not to come to the hospital. The hospital is closed to visitors right now because there are so many people being treated, but luckily, since I came in with the injured, I'm allowed to stay.

When I got back to the waiting room, Micah's gone.

Did something happen? I race down the hall to the room where they moved Ava and Laurel after they came out of surgery, and there's Micah, sitting next to Ava and holding her hand. Their heads are really close together and they're smiling at each other and it's kind of weird, but I ignore them to focus on my mate.

Laurel's lying in the bed closest to the door. Her eyes are still closed and she looks like an angel lying there, just like always. When the doctor sees me, he raises his eyebrows. "Mr Miller, I told you we'd tell you when we had any news."

Micah growls at him, and I'm surprised at the authority he's giving off. "Doctor, that's his mate. Tell him what he needs to know."

And to my surprise, the doctor bows his head at Micah. "Yes, Beta."

Beta? Micah's the Beta now? Clearly I missed a few things, but again, it's not my main worry right now.

The doctor turns to me. "As you already know, your mate was knocked out during the attack. Her physical injuries are fairly minor, but she hasn't regained consciousness yet and we're not sure why."

"Can I talk to her?"

The doctor glances over at Micah who nods firmly, so the doctor agrees. "I'm going to go check on some other patients. Excuse me."

He leaves the room and I take a seat next to Laurel. She's got a different scent about her tonight, and I wonder if it's to do with her injury. But as I take her hand to start talking to her, sparks light up my skin, and suddenly, I understand.

"The mate bond is fixed?" I ask Micah and Ava. They're still grinning at each other, and that finally makes sense too. "You guys are mates?"

They nod at me, and I look down at Laurel with excitement. We're mates too then. Not just chosen mates, but real, destined mates too.

I knew it. I always knew it. We chose each other, but we were meant for each other too. I can't wait to see her face when she realizes it.

Hey, Blaze, I call my wolf in my head. *Can you try to reach Laurel's wolf? Maybe she's conscious even if Laurel isn't.*

He agrees and less than a minute later, he's howling gleefully in my head. *She's our mate! She feels it too.*

I knew she would. *Can she talk to Laurel?*

She'll try, he promises.

I rub her hand, whispering encouragement to her, each second feeling like a lifetime, but finally, her eyelids flutter.

"Laurel? Can you hear me?"

It takes a few seconds longer, but eventually, she smiles and her eyes open, so full of love for me I can hardly stand it. "I hear you, and I smell you too. My mate."

"I told you," I remind her, and we both laugh before I lean down and kiss her. Finally, everything is the way it was always meant to be.

Chapter Twenty-Two

~~Sadie's PoV~~

Everyone else leaves, taking Micah's dad's body with them, and I turn back to Logan a little shyly. He's standing there completely naked, and even though I know I shouldn't, I can't help glancing down at him.

When I lift my eyes again, he's smiling at me, his eyebrows raised. "Really, Sadie? You couldn't wait a few more days?"

"What do you mean?" The way he's looking at me makes my heart race.

"I mean, it's your 18th birthday in a few days," he reminds me. "And then I can claim you properly as my mate, with everything that involves."

He steps closer to me, his scent flooding my senses. He smells like rain and the ocean, a smell I could definitely drown in.

"You want to wait until then?" I can't help asking, and he laughs.

"I don't *want* to, trust me. But I want to do everything right with you, Sadie. Now that I know you were always meant to be mine, I want it to be perfect."

My heart twinges a little. Even after everything that's happened tonight, even after me finally accepting the Moon Goddess' fate for me, it stings to hear him say that he wouldn't have chosen me otherwise.

Logan seems to feel my uncertainty. "Shit, no, that's not what I meant." He runs a hand through his hair in frustration. "Why do I always say the wrong thing? I swear I'll get better at this, Sadie. I just meant, I was going to make you mine anyway. but now that I know it was meant to be, it makes it even better."

"Really?" I want to believe him, but it seems so unlikely after everything we talked about before. "You were really going to choose me?"

"I really was," he promises. "And you were going to choose me, right?"

"I guess we'll never know," I tease him. Someday, I'll tell him everything that happened with Selene and why I made the choice I did. But not tonight. Tonight, we've both been through enough already.

He talks me through how to shift, and it's honestly not as hard as I expected. Ebony does most of the work. I just have to let her take control of my body, *our* body, and once she does, she initiates the shift herself. It hurts like hell, especially since I'm still healing from my wounds, and once we're in our wolf body, it's the weirdest thing I have ever experienced. My eyesight is sharper, my ears hear better and I can smell a million more things than before, but Logan's scent is still the strongest of all. It feels like I could find him from miles away.

Let's go, he says to me in my head after he turns into his wolf too, and together, we run back through the woods, our pace in perfect sync.

He takes me back to my aunt and uncle's house. When we get to the front door, he speaks in my head again.

Stay there, I'll get the door open.

He shifts back to his human form and knocks on the door. My aunt opens it and she looks like she's been crying. "Logan? Do you have any news about Ava?"

Ava? What's happened to Ava? I don't have any idea what she's talking about, but Logan seems to. "She's at the hospital, they're just operating now. Aaron's there with her, he'll update you as soon as he can. For now, can I leave Sadie with you? I'll be back to see her in the morning, but I think after everything, she could use a good night's sleep in her own bed."

"Sadie?" My aunt looks down at my wolf in shock. "But... how?"

"I don't entirely know," Logan admits, and I realize there's still more I need to tell him. "There's going to be a lot to sort through in the morning."

He crouches down, looking straight into my wolf's eyes.

"I'll see you tomorrow, Sadie."

I nod at him and he strokes my fur, sending little sparks flying through me again, and he shifts back into his wolf and heads off back to the pack house. I have a feeling his night isn't over yet, but he's right about one thing. Now that it's all over, I'm absolutely exhausted.

My aunt takes me upstairs and makes sure I get shifted back to my human body okay. I know she has a lot of questions, but she's also distracted about Ava, so when the phone rings, I tell her to go and I'll see her in the morning.

It doesn't take long at all before I fall into the deepest sleep of my life.

~~Logan's PoV~~

My dad gives all of the senior class the next week off school. Most of us were involved in the fighting, and some people are still in the hospital. I spend a lot of time with my dad and Micah, his new Beta. We have to root out everyone that was working with Beta Aldric. It's unpleasant work, especially learning just how many of our pack have betrayed us. I can see how much it bothers my dad. But there's a new peace in his eyes too, knowing that the person responsible for my mom and Kara's death has finally been caught, and I feel lighter too.

Although a lot of that could also be because of my new mate.

I see Sadie as much as I can, but she's at the hospital with Ava a lot, and Micah is too. He told me the morning after the fight that they're mates.

"I never would have guessed," I admit.

He shrugs. "Me neither, but it feels right."

I know what that feels like, which reminds me of the other thing I wanted to talk to him about. "I never knew you had any kind of feelings for Sadie." We haven't talked about this yet, but I figure it's better to clear the air.

"I didn't know you did either," he says.

I nod. That's what I thought. "Is this going to make things weird with us?"

I'm relieved when he shakes his head. "No. To be honest, I thought it would. When she told me you guys were mates, I didn't see how we could move forward from that. But then I felt Ava's fear when she woke up, and I just knew. She needs me, and I don't know if I could have been the man she needs if I hadn't gone through everything with Sadie. I guess it was all meant to happen just the way it did. Who the fuck can say?"

I laugh. "That was almost poetic, right up until the end."

He laughs too. "Yeah, well, I can't totally change, right? Then it wouldn't be me anymore."

"I think you've changed just the right amount," I tell him. "Thank you for everything you did. Sadie wouldn't be here without you."

He shrugs like it's no big deal, but I can see in his eyes that he appreciates the thanks anyway.

Now, it's Wednesday and it's Sadie's birthday. My dad insisted that she have a big party. He says it will be good for the pack to have something to celebrate. He's one of only a few people who know that she's my mate. We don't want to have to explain to everyone why she got her wolf early or that she's the vessel. The fewer people that know about that, the better. All my dad has shared with the pack is that Beta Aldric was a traitor, we defeated him and the mate bonds have been restored.

Sadie has told me everything though. She told me about how the Moon Goddess came to her and about the choice she was given. At first, I was a little hurt that she didn't choose me when she had the chance, but when she explained to me why she didn't, that she didn't want me to ever feel that she had tricked me into anything, I could understand her reasoning. I promised her once again that I really was going to choose her no matter what, but that knowing she was always meant for me really does make everything better.

I have a gift for her for her party tonight, and I have plans for us later. I can't wait to acknowledge her as my mate in front of everyone and make it fully official later.

Everyone gathers again on the back lawn of the pack house, just like they did for my birthday last week. We even reused a lot of the same decorations. I know Sadie won't mind. She's not the kind of person to get bothered about things like that.

I'm wearing a suit. I know Sadie will be dressed up and I want us to look good together. It's the first time I'm seeing a lot of the pack since everything that happened on Friday, and they all thank me for taking the lead while my dad was injured and keeping the pack safe. I tell them it's what I had to do, but I appreciate their support anyway.

When Micah and Ava come in, everyone turns to look at them. Ava's wearing a pretty white flowy dress that covers her legs completely as she sits in her wheelchair. Micah stands proudly beside her, but a little defensively, as if he's daring anyone to look at her the wrong way.

I go over and say hi to them both. I've been to visit Ava in the hospital a few times, and I still feel guilty about her injuries even though she told me she doesn't blame me. We lost three wolves that night, and there are a few seriously injured still, like Ava, and I can't help but feel responsible. They were all under my command. My dad promises it will get easier over time, and I have to trust he's right. Right now, it still feels like crap.

"Somebody dressed up," Ava teases me as I lean down to kiss her cheek. She's one of the few who already knows about Sadie being my mate.

"I couldn't let her totally outshine me," I reply. "Like you and Micah. No one would believe he's worthy of you."

"Thanks, Logan," Micah says sarcastically, and we all laugh. I feel like this is a small glimpse into our future, me and my Beta, our mates, living here in the pack house, running the pack. If this is what it'll be like, I think it's going to be pretty great.

A hushed gasp sweeps through the crowd, and I know before I even turn that Sadie has arrived. I can smell her sweet scent and feel her nearness on my skin.

And when I turn and see her, the whole rest of the world just fades away. She's wearing a pale violet dress, her dark hair half pulled back just like it was the day we met in the cafeteria, and I can't help sending up a silent thank you to the Moon Goddess, who I'm certain is watching us tonight.

Thank you for making her mine.

~~Sadie's PoV~~

The lawn is full of people but I can only see one of them. Logan looks incredibly sexy in his suit. It strains against his broad shoulders, like whoever made it hadn't anticipated someone built like him ever trying to wear it, but it's the look on his face that really takes my breath away. He looks at me like I'm the most precious gift he could ever get. I will never get tired of seeing that look.

I had a little cry in my room earlier when I was getting ready. I cried for my parents, that they wouldn't be there for this night and that they would never get to meet my wonderful mate. I cried for Logan's mom and sister too, that their lives were cut painfully short by the twisted man who tried to kill me too.

And I cried for Ava, that she won't be able to dance with me tonight. The doctors are still hopeful that she might make a full recovery and she's in pretty good spirits. It helps that Micah is being amazing with her. I'm so proud of him, and happy for them both. He and I had a good talk earlier and I feel like we're good now. I think the four of us will all be good together.

And now that I see Logan looking at me like that, the tears start to come back to my eyes, but I quickly blink them away. This is not a night to be sad. This is the night that the rest of my life starts, this life I never expected or even thought I wanted.

This is the night I truly claim my wolf.

We go through the usual rituals that I'm starting to see are normal for these kinds of nights. When the sun sets, the Alpha calls me up to the raised platform with him.

I step up with him in front of the whole pack, *my* pack, as the Alpha takes my hand and gives me a warm smile.

"You haven't been in Westbridge very long, Sadie," he says, speaking loudly enough that everyone can hear. "But things have certainly been interesting since you got here."

There is a murmured agreement among the crowd, and I can't help blushing. "I hope it's a lot less interesting from here on in, Alpha."

He laughs and others do too. "None of us know what the future brings," he reminds me. "But it is my honor to welcome you as a full member of the Westbridge pack. Now, do you see your mate in the crowd?"

He gives me a private wink, since he already knows exactly who it is. And when I turn to the crowd, Logan is front and center. "Mate," he calls out, and several people in the crowd gasp in surprise.

"Mate," I agree, nodding at him and smiling, and he runs up to the platform, taking me in his arms in front of everyone and placing a sweet, lingering kiss on my lips.

"Sadie and Logan!" the Alpha announces and the whole pack applauds, making me blush once again. Logan laughs at the color in my cheeks and he keeps his arm around me as we both acknowledge the crowd.

Then it's time for me to shift, which isn't scary at all since I've done it several times already now. Logan tells me my wolf is a charcoal color, black like the ebony my wolf is named for, but with a bit of moonglow, just right for the goddess' vessel. I don't know if that's on purpose or not, and neither does he, but he tells me I'm beautiful in either form.

We stay at the party a while longer and Logan gives me a present, a beautiful necklace with two halves of a heart on it.

"Is this for us?" I ask him, fingering the little heart pieces.

"Not exactly," he explains, and I frown until he elaborates further. "It was my mother's. I remember I asked her about it once and she said it was for her and her best friend. I think now that it must have been your mom."

Tears threaten to spill out again as I look at the beautiful, thoughtful gift, and I kiss him, not caring that everyone can see us. There are some catcalls and whistles, and this time it's Logan who's blushing when I pull away.

"I'm going inside now," he whispers in my ear. "Come and see me whenever you're ready."

A shiver of anticipation runs through me as he walks away. I force myself to stay a while longer to talk to the people who are waiting to see me, their future Luna, but eventually I can't wait any longer. I sneak away and head up the stairs to the room that I know is Logan's.

I knock quietly and the door opens almost immediately, like he was waiting for me on the other side. His body blocks the entry as he opens it just a crack. "Hey."

"Hey, yourself," I reply. "Are you going to let me in?"

He grins and steps back, opening the door all the way, and my mouth falls open. The whole room is decorated with candles and rose petals, like something out of a movie.

"You did all this for me?"

"I don't know how good this is going to be," he admits, biting his lip a little nervously. "I wanted you to have at least some good memories of tonight."

His uncertainty makes my heart melt. "It's going to be great," I promise him. "Just because it's you."

He pulls me further inside, closing the door behind us, and takes me in his arms again. "I'm so glad you came here, Sadie," he whispers to me. "You brought me back to life again."

"You helped me so much too," I tell him. "I couldn't have gotten through all of this without you."

He smiles. "I think you could have. You're so strong."

"So are you."

"I love you, Sadie." His words are feather-soft, barely more than a whisper, but they mean everything to me.

"I love you too, Logan."

We take our time getting undressed. Last week, when we were in here making out, it was rushed and hurried, but tonight, it feels like we have all the time in the world. I take off his suit jacket, his tie, and his dress shirt, then I kiss my way along his broad chest. His eyes close at my touch, feeling the sparks between us.

He unzips my dress, and as it falls to the floor, his eyes widen at the sight. Ava helped me pick out the sexiest set of underwear that we could have delivered here before tonight, and apparently, it was worth the effort.

"I'm so goddamn lucky," he murmurs as he bends down to kiss the top of my breasts that swell above the bra.

I feel like the lucky one right now. Every touch of his lips or fingers is like magic. He helps me down onto the bed, onto the pile of soft rose petals he arranged on it, and takes off his pants. I can already see the hard outline of his cock through his underwear, looking so much bigger already than it did the other night in the woods when I took a peek at it.

Logan seems to read my mind. "I wasn't turned on that night," he tells me. "Not like I am now, seeing you on my bed like this."

He pulls his underwear off and I have to remember to breathe as I finally see just how big and hard he really is.

I reach out to touch him, but he shakes his head at me. "Not yet. I need to see you first."

He gently helps me out of my underwear until I'm just as naked as he is. Nobody's ever seen me like this before but I don't feel shy. I only want to be with him.

Still, we take our time, touching and exploring each other. I love when he inhales at my touch, letting me know how it affects him. I moan as he kisses my breasts, sucking on the nipples, and when his fingers move between my legs, a shock of pleasure runs through me.

"Is that good?" he asks quickly, surprised at the way my body tenses.

"So good," I assure him. "Don't stop."

He doesn't. He runs his fingers through my wetness, finding the little bud there that makes me quiver again, and then, very gently, he presses his fingers inside me. I cry out in amazement. It feels so good, the sparks travelling up inside me, but it's not enough. I want more.

Once again, he reads my mind. "Is it okay if I…"

"Yes, please. Let me feel you, Logan."

It's a little awkward, I won't lie. Neither of us know exactly what we're doing, but eventually we find the right position, the place where we fit together just perfectly, and as he pushes into me, we both shudder with the absolute rightness of it.

He stops only a short way in. "I think this is the part that's going to hurt, Sadie."

He looks so worried that I reach up to give him a kiss. "I know. It's okay."

Logan doesn't look like he agrees, but we couldn't stop now even if we wanted to, and we definitely don't want to. I whimper a little at the strange feeling inside me and he grimaces at the sound. "Fuck, I'm sorry."

He keeps going though, and soon, he's all the way in and I've never felt so complete before in all my life.

I thought I'd found where I was meant to be, here in this pack, but now I know that was only part of it. *This* is where I'm meant to be, here in Logan's arms, joined together in the most intimate way, our hearts beating in perfect sync.

He rests there a moment until I'm ready to keep going, and it doesn't take long. With the sparks flying between us, his fingers exploring my clit as he thrusts into me, and the perfect feeling of belonging with him, my pleasure builds, faster and faster, until I feel like I'm going to explode.

And then... I do. The build-up suddenly bursts and all I'm left with is pleasure and satisfaction, rushing through every fiber of my body. When he shudders on top of me, I know he's felt it too.

Mate, Ebony calls out.

I know, I answer her breathlessly in my head.

No, she counters. *Make him our mate. Mark him!*

Oh, right. I don't really know how to do that, and yet, somehow, I do. Moving purely by instinct, I pull Logan's neck towards me and my teeth grow longer, my wolf form coming out just in my mouth, and I sink the sharp canines into the sweet spot on his neck.

Logan calls out my name, his voice joyful, and as soon as I've finished, he does the same to me, marking me as his, now and forever.

When we fall back onto the pillows together, I look at the mark I've just made on him, running my fingers over it.

"You've claimed me," he teases, but his eyes are shining with love. "I'm yours now."

"And I'm yours," I remind him, snuggling into his warm, solid body. "Me and my wolf. You've claimed us too."

~~The End~~

THANK YOU

If you enjoyed this book, please take a moment to leave a review!

You can find more of my books as below. For all the latest news, please follow me on Facebook or join the reader group, The Four Muses. All the links are on my Linktree: linktr.ee/jadeember

Claiming My Wolf - Dreame (ebook) and Amazon (paperback)

<u>*Werewolf Empire Series*</u>
Blind Dating the Alpha Prince - Dreame (ebook) and Amazon (paperback)
Twisted Bonds - all ebook retailers and Amazon (paperback)

<u>*Out of Time Series*</u>
The Last Wolf Prince – Dreame (ebook) and Amazon (paperback)
Out of Time - all ebook retailers and Amazon (paperback)